MANIFEST

A Mystyx Novel

MANIFEST

A Mystyx Novel

ARTIST ARTHUR

KIMANI
TRU
™

Recycling programs
for this product may
not exist in your area.

MANIFEST: A MYSTYX NOVEL

ISBN-13: 978-0-373-83196-8

© 2010 by Artist Arthur

www.KimaniTRU.com

Printed in U.S.A.

To Asia D. Arthur:
"Teen Queen" of my household,
God has big plans for you.

Acknowledgments

Thank you Jesus, for never giving up on me.

To Mrs. Rosanna Miles: Leading Lady of the Koinonia Baptist Church, thanks for being "psychic." Next time I'll listen sooner.

To Traneika S. Fleet: adults can be stubborn too. You requested a young adult story a while ago. I hope this lives up to your expectations.

To the "Wonder Woman" of literary agents, Christine Witthohn. Thanks for believing in me long before we had this chance to work together.

To *Family Matters,* for being the family that matters to me.

To my church family, my Kimani family and the literary divas who have become a great support to me—Gwyneth Bolton, Adrianne Byrd and Maureen Smith—much gratitude and hugs and kisses to you all.

And last, but certainly not least, to Damon, Andre, Asia and Amaya—the best promotional team a wife and mother could ever ask for.

Dear Reader,

In *Manifest,* the first book in the Mystyx series, you will meet Krystal Bentley, a fifteen-year-old who finds herself not only dealing with the drama of being the new girl in school, but also finding out some pretty unbelievable things about herself.

Krystal is your average teenager, or at least that's what she wants to believe. The fact that she can see, hear and talk to ghosts is something she'd like to ignore. Making new friends is usually what happens when you move to a new town and attend a new school. But for Krystal, the first friend she meets is a ghost named Ricky, who needs her help. The next friends she makes seem weird, but they all share the same M-shaped birthmark, which can't be a coincidence.

Seems like a lot to swallow all at once? Yeah, that's how Krystal's feeling right about now. But as time goes on Krystal learns to accept her "abilities" and the new family situation that is thrust upon her. The unexpected happiness at finding a new boyfriend is icing on the cake.

Manifest is Krystal's story. It follows her efforts to navigate the ordinary problems every teen faces growing up, as well as trying to figure out where she fits in with the Mystyx. I hope you enjoy Krystal's story, and stay tuned for the next Mystyx novel as her friends deal with their own problems and special powers.

Enjoy,

Artist

Tonight I will die.

They have decided to kill me.

They call themselves religious and me the devil. But they are the evil ones. They are the ones with the power to judge and to kill.

He's coming now, I can hear his footsteps. Slow. Heavy. Closer.

I am not what they say. My soul is not touched by the evil. I am as pure as they.

He's here now, his keys clanking against metal. I'm scared. I can say that now, here on this parchment as the words in my mind print in ink while my hands are still tucked inside the torn pockets of my shirt. I don't know how or why I can do this.

They say it is the darkness within me, the darkness that they fear.

Mary Burroughs
Salem Town, Massachusetts
15 May 1692

one

"**I can't** hear you. I can't hear you," I repeat, talking to myself. Maybe if I keep saying it the voice will go away. I know people driving by me probably think I'm a lunatic.

My feet are moving so fast I barely feel them touch the ground. Cool air slaps my face like it's trying to remind me that I'm outside. It's almost spring according to the calendar, but it still feels like the dead of winter in Lincoln. Probably because we're so close to the water.

Whatever. I'm cold and I think it's beginning to rain. But I don't care. I just want to get home, inside the house, to the safety of my room. It won't follow me there.

I can't *believe* it followed me here. I ignored *it* in New York. You'd think *it* would have the good sense to stay in the city where there's a little excitement. Why follow me here to the ends of the earth where everyone acts like they're sleepwalking most of the time?

As I cut through the bushes at the end of the driveway, my book bag sways back and forth, threatening to slide off my shoulder as I run. If it does, my Biology book will fall out and the hastily scribbled notes I took this morning on the project that's due at the end of the month will probably hit the ground and blow away. That might not be such a bad thing.

I hunch my shoulders, pushing the book bag back into place. My feet crush the weeds in the flower bed that Janet will likely replant in a few weeks. And I keep running.

My cheeks puff in and out as I inhale huge gulps of air to keep my heart pumping. I'm not a runner. Actually, I hate exercise of any kind and it shows. I take the front steps two at a time because I want to hurry up and get to my room.

Help me.

Damn! There it goes again.

I press the palm of my hand over my ear while I dig in my front pocket for the house key. My fingers are shaking but I finally get the door unlocked, slam it shut behind me and take the stairs in the front hall like a steroid-pumped-up Olympic sprinter.

My room is at the far end of the hall, but I swear it feels like it's twenty miles away as I dash toward the door. Once inside, I slam the door, drop my book bag and sink to the floor struggling to breathe.

Safe. All I can think is that I'm finally safe.

Help me.

His voice echoes around the room, louder than it was before. Louder than when I was on the school bus or when I was running into the house.

It's been a long time. I thought this creepy stuff was over. I haven't heard voices since I was twelve years old, and I'm not sure if I really heard them then.

Who am I kidding? I heard them before and now they're back. But I cover my ears because I want the voice to stop so badly.

I'm rocking on the floor now, pulling my knees to my chest and wrapping my arms around them, holding myself tightly. My eyes are closed. I wish I could find a way to close my ears, too.

I did it before. I quieted the voices for a long, long time. But now they're back. Why?

"I can't hear you. I can't see you. You are not real."

But I *can* hear him, that's the freakin' problem.

Help me, Krystal.

"I can't hear you. I can't see you. You are not—"

Did he say my name?

Please, he begs.

For some reason the sound of his voice isn't scaring me anymore. I loosen my grip around my legs and I stop rocking. My heart still feels like it's going to jump out of my chest and land on the floor, but for some reason I'm not scared now.

I open my eyes, not that I mean to, it just happens I guess. I look toward the window seat where all the stupid stuffed animals Janet thought would cheer me up are arrayed like a pastel-colored army.

I don't know what I'm looking for. Whatever it is, I hope I don't find it.

But there he is—a black boy, kind of tall and skinny. He's wearing jeans, the baggy kind like all the guys in school wear, and a white T-shirt three sizes too big, hanging to his knees like a nightgown. His boots look new, Timberlands with the laces only halfway up, the huge tongue sticking out from the sagging denim hem of his jeans. He's wearing a watch on one wrist and a bracelet—I think it's silver— on the other. His hair is kind of curly on top, cut low on the sides with some lines or a design or something.

I suppose he's kind of cute.

But he's kind of transparent.

two

DINNER sucks.

For one, Janet, my mother, can't cook. How do you burn boiled eggs? Janet knows how and the smell is awful. But that was a few weeks ago.

Tonight's culinary masterpiece is spaghetti. Again, shouldn't be too hard. Drop some pasta in water, let it boil, open up a jar of sauce and you're done.

Not!

What's on the plate in front of me is some soupy mess that I'm really afraid to eat. So instead I pick the cucumbers out of my salad because I don't like them. She knows I don't like them but she keeps right on putting them in my salad.

"So, how was school today?" she asks like she's a real mom or something.

Okay, well, maybe I'm being harsh. She did give birth to me and she does make sure there's a roof over my head and food—well, two out of three ain't bad.

Her one fault, for which I am resigned to be pissed at her for the next ten to twenty years of my life, is that she divorced my father and moved me from New York City to this *Little House on the Prairie* town in Connecticut.

Bottom line, I'm just not feeling my mother right now. But that's not what's really bothering me. I can't stop thinking about the boy upstairs in my room.

I was just about to ask him who he was and why he was following me around when Janet called me for dinner. I could have stalled and made up some excuse, but that just would have delayed this joyous family meal.

"School was fine," I say hurriedly, because she's looking at me like she wants to ask even more questions.

Janet is still pretty, even though she's old. I think anyone over thirty is old. Janet is thirty-five. She had me when she was twenty, before she could graduate from college. My father is ten years older than her. She has really long, wavy, black hair and her skin isn't as dark as mine. She's half Cherokee.

I'm only one-quarter Cherokee because I'm mixed with her and my father and he's just black. My hair is pretty nice; it doesn't get all nappy when I sweat like some of my cousins' hair. It just looks bushy and puffy like one of those puppies that I can never remember the name of.

Anyway, I don't want to sit here at the dinner table with all these dishes and Janet on one side and an empty chair where her new husband, Gerald, usually sits on the other side.

Gerald comes home late mostly every night because he works for some international company that does business in different time zones—that's what Janet says. I think he's probably at work screwing his secretary or something. Or maybe he just wants to be anyplace I'm not.

When he met Janet she didn't tell him about me right away. I don't know why. I overheard them one time talking about which parent it would be best for me to live with. Gerald didn't act like he wanted it to be Janet. On that one thing, he and I both agree.

"There's a spring dance coming up. We could go buy you

a pretty new dress," Janet says, trying to twirl the flat, sticky spaghetti onto her fork.

"I don't want a new dress," I say adamantly, because I don't. I don't like dresses.

"Then we could just find you a nice outfit to wear."

"I'm probably not going to go."

"Why?"

"Because I don't know any boys?" *Unless you count the one waiting for me upstairs.* The one I'm hesitant to call a ghost.

Because if I actually admit that's what he is, then I might as well pack my bags and head to the loony bin.

"You've been here for months and the school year is almost over. You haven't made any friends?"

I shrug because I don't really think it's a big deal. I like being alone. That way I don't have to explain the things about me that even I don't understand.

"I don't need friends."

She sighs. "Everybody needs somebody, Krystal."

"You didn't need Daddy," I snap. I immediately regret my tone of voice and I clamp my mouth shut. The fork that was stabbing at cucumbers falls from my hand, making a clanking sound on the plate.

"What happened between your father and me had nothing to do with you," she says slowly, not looking at me.

Anytime she talks about my father, which isn't often, she doesn't look at me. Like she can't even face what she's done to me.

"I'm just supposed to suffer because of it," I yell, standing and pushing my chair back from the table until it falls to the floor.

Janet reaches out until her hand touches my wrist. "I don't want you to suffer, honey. I want you to be happy and healthy. But you're not eating, you're not socializing. You're not talking."

I snatch my arm away. Her words are true even if I don't want to admit it. I don't really have an appetite anymore and I don't talk because I have nobody to talk to. But that's not my fault. A year ago I had all that. I could eat half a large pepperoni pizza with extra cheese all by myself. I had friends from school, or at least people I socialized with— even if only on a limited basis. But I had them. Now I'm alone.

"I don't need anybody."

Janet stands and comes closer to me. "Listen, Krystal. If you want to go and see someone, a psychiatrist or—"

"Oh, great! That is so whack. Send me to a shrink because you don't want to listen to me."

I'm stalking across the room now, not wanting her to touch me or say anything to me, or sense the pain this entire situation is causing in the pit of my stomach. How did she expect me to eat with that burning bubble always wrenching inside me?

"It's not that I don't want to listen, Krys. You don't want to talk to me."

"You're right!" I say, spinning around to face her one more time. "I don't want to talk to you. I don't want to talk to anybody."

I'm running up the stairs again. It feels like déjà vu. Only this time when I close my bedroom door it's not his voice I hear but his presence I feel.

three

It's like somebody put a sweater around my arms. I shiver even though I didn't realize I was cold. I'm in the house. It's raining outside but it's dry and warm inside. Goose bumps still prickle the bare skin on my arms.

In the pit of my stomach it feels like butterflies are dancing around. That's strange because just a few minutes ago, downstairs with Janet, I felt that same burning in my stomach that I feel whenever I'm around her—whenever I think of her leaving my father.

I rest my forehead on the door, afraid to turn around, afraid not to.

He's here, the boy. I know he is even though he's not calling my name or begging me to help him.

What should I do?

I could scream and Janet would come running. But what would she see? I don't think she can see ghosts. I didn't think I could either.

The funny thing is I'd convinced myself I was cursed or crazy or both when I heard the voices before. The first time was when I was five. The last time I was twelve and had gone to visit my grandfather—on my father's side—in a nursing home. I figured the voice was one of the old people asking for help or for food or the sound of someone who simply wanted a hug.

That night I swore I'd never hear another voice and for a while I thought my vow had worked.

Until today.

How long are you going to stand there?

His voice sounds so normal, like he's just a boy from school sitting in my room talking to me.

I press my palms against the door and take a deep breath. I'm already in my room, my safe place. There is nowhere else for me to run or hide.

So, I figure I just better face it, I'm crazy.

I turn slowly and look toward the window seat. He's sitting there, his back to the wall, one leg propped up on the seat cushion. My stuffed animal army is on the floor. Can dead people move things?

"What do you want?" I ask in the same monotone he uses. For some reason I don't feel nervous, just tired. Of running or ignoring the voice, I guess.

I need your help.

"I can't help you."

You don't even know what I need you to do.

"Well, you're dead, right? I can't bring you back to life." I'm not *that* crazy.

He sighs, like I'm getting on his nerves.

I don't want to come back, he says then stops like he's thinking about his words. *I just need some answers. I need to find out who did this to me.*

"Then you should go to the police or a lawyer. I don't know, just stop stalking me."

He chuckles. *Stalking or haunting?*

I don't find the situation very funny. "Just go."

I can't. Not yet. They think somebody from my crew killed me. But that's not true.

Suddenly I'm really sleepy. I feel like I've been up for

hours. I hear the words coming out of his mouth—unfortunately—but I'm too tired to comprehend them. I move away from the door and trudge over to my bed where I plop down and stare at the ceiling.

"Who's your crew? No, first, who are you?"

My name is Ricky Watson. I used to go to Settlemans High until last year when I was shot in the alley behind the school.

I think I've heard the name.

"Your brother is Antoine Watson?"

Yeah, he's a year younger than me. He's in the tenth grade now. I was a junior.

"Did you ask him for help?"

You're the only one who can hear me.

"I was afraid of that."

I drape my arm over my forehead and close my eyes. I don't want to see him but my eyes feel like they're going to turn toward him on their own. So I cover them.

"I don't want to hear you," I say because it's the truth.

That's cool. But you can. And if you can hear me, you can help.

"What if I don't want to? What will happen then?"

I won't go where I'm supposed to.

"And where's that?"

Not sure. But I know I wouldn't still be here talking to you if there wasn't something I needed to do.

"How do you know that?"

He chuckles again. I think I like the sound of his voice now.

I used to watch a lot of those shows on TV that talk about dead people not crossing over, having unfinished business and all that.

My arm slides from my eyes and I turn my head. He's still sitting in the window seat. Ricky Watson—the dead boy. He has a dimple in his left cheek.

"This is crazy. I must be crazy," I say, keeping my eyes on him. "I'm lying in my room talking to a ghost."

You know, the crazy part is that I'm dead and still can't get any peace.

I close my eyes because my lids feel really heavy. Then something happens. I feel something.

It's warm and soft and those butterflies in my stomach dance around some more. I open my eyes slowly and Ricky isn't in the window seat. He's standing right next to my bed now, his hand hovering over my face.

It's really close, Ricky's hand. I can see the lines in the palm of his hand, the ones my grandmother used to tell me told your future. He acts like he's brushing my hair aside, but it doesn't really feel like it.

Go to sleep. We'll get started tomorrow.

He's talking to me like my father, or an older brother I guess. His hand is still moving across my body but I don't really feel like I'm being touched.

I feel like my body is becoming warm.

I'm back again, inside the dream.

I know this place.

It's our apartment in New York. I inhale deeply and my mouth waters so I lick my lips. Daddy's frying chicken.

He's from the South, my father. Calvin Jefferson Bentley. His parents were born and raised in Charleston, South Carolina. When he graduated from high school he went to college in New York, said he always wanted to live in the Big Apple. That's where he met my mother, but that was years later since he's ten years older than her.

All I know is he makes the best fried chicken and my stomach is growling. I feel like I haven't eaten in months.

Twelve months to be exact.

In my dream, I open the door and leave my bedroom. It's painted blue, my favorite color, and I love just looking at the walls and the matching curtains. But right now I don't mind leaving so much.

There's a short hallway then I'm in the living room. The TV is on, tuned to a sports channel. Daddy loves his sports.

I can hear the fried chicken sizzling and see trails of smoke traveling through the air. I keep moving, letting my stomach be my guide.

Just as I thought, on the stove is a deep cast-iron frying pan that looks like it will knock you out if somebody was fool enough to hit you with it. Inside the pan are a couple pieces of chicken, sitting in the hot bubbling cooking oil turning a golden-brown color.

On a plate across the counter from the stove is more chicken piled high like a pyramid. I don't waste a minute. I hurry over, pick up a breast because I love the white meat and put it to my lips.

As I take that first bite, juice dripping down my chin, the warm, greasy, spicy taste moving around my mouth as I chew, I hear the door slam. So I turn around. I'm still carrying my piece of chicken and chewing as I enter the living room.

The TV is off now. There are suitcases by the door. I recognize the bags. They are dark blue with goldfish airport tags that I saved from our trip to SeaWorld a few years ago.

I swallow my bite of chicken but it sort of gets stuck in my throat as I look around the room and cough.

The big picture of Mama and Daddy the day they got married is gone. It usually sits on the sofa table in a big crystal frame. Not anymore.

Mama loves elephants. She collects them and puts them all around the apartment. They're gone, too.

Moving like I'm in a trance, I head to my room, push open the door and drop the chicken breast on the floor. It's empty. The walls are still blue, the curtains are still at the window, but all my stuff is gone. My posters of Beyoncé and T.I.—gone. My *Twilight* calendar—gone. My gray pullover Aeropostle hoodie that I always keep on the closet doorknob—that's right—gone.

My eyes are burning with tears as I remember why everything is gone. It hits me full force, the conversation with Mama as we boarded the train that would take us away from the city. The calm way that she told me she was leaving Daddy for good and taking me back to her hometown.

I don't want to go to the small town where she grew up. I don't want to leave the city. I don't want to leave Daddy.

So I turn away. I try to run. My feet move fast. I'm always running. I keep running and running until I trip over something and fall.

It's raining again. It always seems to be raining. My fingers tighten into a fist and I feel cool wet mud under my nails. I hate the dirt and struggle to stand up, but when I do I'm confused.

I'm no longer in the apartment.

It's dark here and foggy. I can't really see anything but stones—rows and rows of stones.

Krystal.

I hear my name and turn in the direction I think it's coming from. I don't see anyone.

Krystal.

There it is again but it's a different voice this time.

Okay, so I don't know where I am, or why I'm out here in the dark cold rain. But I know it's not where I want to be so I start to walk fast. Then I bump into one of the stones.

I scream because pain ricochets through my body when it slams into my kneecap. I'm bending over rubbing my knee when I look up and read the stone directly in front of me.

Ricardo Watson
March 4, 1993–February 7, 2009

My heart beats wildly in my chest. I touch my heart—through my shirt, of course—thinking I can slow my heartbeat as I stand.

Krystal.

This time the voice is familiar. But when I turn toward it, I don't see anybody. I don't see Ricky.

It's eerily dark but there's, like, this mist hovering above the stones. I take another painful step when I hear my name again. Okay, to hell with the steps. I break into a run only to be stopped short by a loud sound, kind of like thunder rolling in the sky. Then the mist grows darker until it's a thick black cloud of smoke that swirls around my ankles, moving upward toward my thighs.

Now my heart feels like it's about to come out of my chest. I'm breathing heavily and my entire body is trembling. My face and neck feel damp, from sweat maybe? Or had it started to rain? I don't know what to do. Don't have a clue why I'm here or what's going on. Should I run? Should I scream?

What is this? What's happening to me?

Finally my mind wraps around the fact that I'd better do something rather than playing Twenty Questions. But just as I take off running I see a bunch of people coming toward me—a bunch of dead people.

four

sleepy and cranky is how I feel when I finally step off the school bus the next morning.

After the nightmare of Ricky's tombstone, I couldn't go back to sleep. I booted up my computer intending to play Bejeweled, but instead watched as my fingers typed the word *supernatural* in the search engine box as if it were a Ouija board.

Tons of sites for a television show popped up, so I figured I needed to be a little more specific. *Supernatural powers.* Click.

Is that what I have?

There is no denying I was seeing ghosts or spirits or whatever you call it. Scrolling down the page, I saw lots of sites that had lots of information. But since I'm seeing dead people, I clicked on the one that said *clairvoyants.*

The ghost talked to me and I heard him and I talked back. That's *clairaudience,* according to the site. *Clairsentience* is when somebody senses the presence and thoughts of the spirit.

And me, I'm reading all this and comparing myself to the people on these blogs. Why? Because that's what crazy people do!

I was interrupted by the bleep of an instant message. Clicking on the small box in the lower left corner of the screen, I wonder who could be sending me a message this time of night.

I haven't gotten any instant messages—aside from those from online chat groups about movies, songs or celebrities—so I was really curious as to who could be sending me one now.

It was from ChicTeen.

Every time I boot up my computer, I'm automatically logged into the ChicTeen site, a chat room with millions of teen members around the world.

To: krystalgem
From: number1
Ur cute :)

What? Okay, now there's something else that's weird. Who is "number1" and how did he or she know I'm cute? For a minute I just drummed my fingers on the desk, watching the cursor flick on and off. The flashing cursor almost looked impatient, like it was waiting for me to type something in. But I didn't know how to respond. I didn't know who it was. I guess either way it's polite to say thanks, so that's what I typed.

Reply: thx

Bleep.

number1: lk ur eyes

Now we're officially in the creepy zone. "Who is this?" I said aloud like I really expected a voice from the computer to answer.

Reply: who r u
number1: a friend

Can you say perv? Jeez, who was this idiot?

Reply: ok friend, thx & gnite

I clicked out of the chat room and shut it down quickly. I didn't want to give "number1" a chance to reply.

Just about then the light began to push through the blinds in my room, signaling that it's time to get ready for school. Clearly, crazy time was over and now it was time to get back to normal again. But then I'm not normal—never have been and probably never will be.

Getting ready for school is a perfunctory exercise for me since what I wear and the way I look aren't a big deal. I always grab what's clean, what's closest and what matches. Then I head to the kitchen for a Pop-Tart and glass of juice before leaving the house—and the stress that surrounds me at home—for a few hours.

Settlemans High is nothing like my old school in New York. It's bigger for one, surrounded on one side by grass and more grass until it runs into tall trees that seem to touch the sky. On the other side is a parking lot, big like the ones at the mall. Students with cars park there, and just about everybody has a car. I don't. The bus is my main mode of transportation.

In the back of the school is another parking lot where the teachers and other staff park. Also the tennis courts, baseball field, stadium and track field are back there. My old school only had a gym and no parking for anybody.

This school isn't as crowded either. There are a bunch

of kids, but only like three hundred compared to the nearly two thousand in New York.

I should stop making comparisons. I'm here now and that's that. Still, my mind keeps tallying up all this information for later use.

He's looking at me the moment I step off the bus. His name is Franklin. He looks at me all the time. And I guess I must look at him, too, otherwise how would I know he's looking at me?

Except today when he looks at me I turn away quickly because I don't want to see him. The boy I want to see is Ricky, I think. But he's conveniently disappeared. That should be a good thing. Maybe he won't come back at all.

I take my usual route to my locker when my cell phone rings. Nobody but Janet and my father have the number so I instantly think there's something wrong. Dropping my book bag in front of the bank of lockers, I reach into my purse to fish it out. Looking at the caller ID, I realize I don't know this number. So I change my mind about answering.

Working the combination lock, I pull open the door to my locker. I start to take out the books I'll need for the three periods before lunch, when I can come back to my locker. But when I stand up to put them inside I kind of gasp because Franklin's standing right there.

"Hi, Krystal," he says and smiles.

"Hey, Franklin," I say, trying not to sound mean when I really want to yell at him for almost scaring the life out of me.

"Need some help?"

"With what? Putting my books in my locker? No, thanks," I reply and know it sounds frosty this time.

Franklin's not bad. I mean, he's not bad to look at or anything so I'm not, like, repulsed to be around him. He's got to be mixed, because his complexion is creamy and his hair is wavy. He's taller than me and always wears polo shirts. A lot of the girls like him. I hear them talking about him in the bathroom and in the cafeteria. But to me, he's just okay. I mean, it's not like I'm looking for a boyfriend. Or even a friend-friend for that matter.

"I can walk you to your class."

"It's right over there."

"I can still walk you," he says when I slam my locker shut.

I shrug because again I'm tired and arguing with him might take up the little bit of energy I have left.

As we're walking my cell phone rings again. "Dang," I swear because it's probably that number again. The one I don't know and have no intention of answering.

Still, I once again pull it from my purse. Yep, it's that same number. I cut off the call.

"Mad at your man?" Franklin asks.

"What?"

He nods toward my purse and the cell phone. "You ducking his calls?"

I shake my head, confused as to why he would even think I had a boyfriend let alone one that I would be trying to ignore. "No. I don't know who that is calling."

"Well, I know it's not me."

"Of course it's not because you're standing right here."

Franklin just smiles as we approach the door that leads to my Biology class. "No, I mean, I know it's not me because I don't have your number."

For a minute I feel like an idiot but then I think he's the one who should feel stupid with that tired line he just tried to use on me.

"So can I have it?" he finally asks.

"Can you have what?" I know what he's talking about this time, but I'm trying to figure out if I should give it to him and then ignore his calls the way I just ignored this other one. Or should I just tell him no. I've never had a boy call me before.

His smile seems to grow bigger, just about all of his white teeth showing. "Can I have your number, Krystal?"

"What do you want it for?" I'm still stalling, trying to make my mind up.

"So I can call you. Why else?"

"And why would you want to call me when you see me every day in school?"

He takes a step closer to me, his smile slipping a little, his eyes glued to mine. "Because I might want to talk to you when we're not in school—you know, in private."

I nod like I understand.

"So, are you going to give me your number?"

I take a deep breath just as the bell rings. "Hope you've got a good memory," I say and then ramble off the number so fast he can't possibly remember it. I walk away and head for class, knowing he has only five minutes to get to wherever his first-period class is or he'll be late.

After I sit down I begin to wonder if he'll remember the number. Then again, why do I care? What will I say when he calls—if he calls? No, forget it. I don't want to talk to him any more than I want to talk to anybody else.

Except Ricky said that we'd get started today. I wonder if that means I'll talk to him again.

Lunch is like organized chaos. The cafeteria is large with its yellow-and-white speckled tile floors and painted cinder block walls. The tables aren't like the long Formica-topped ones in elementary and middle school. Instead they are real tables with plastic chairs that are scattered about. As at most high schools, there's a cool-students side and a not-so-cool-students side. In the left corner near the fruit juice machine, that always stays full because if given the choice kids will definitely choose a soda before something that says "100% fruit juice," the goths, geeks and any other looks, style or financially challenged students sit.

It's weird, this class system here in Lincoln, Connecticut. Not weird in the sense that my school back in New York didn't have student segregation, but in that most of these kids are segregated based on the neighborhood they live in.

Take, for instance, Chloe Delaney. She lives right near Sea Point, which has huge houses with decks and private boat docks. She's a Richie and she sits on the right-hand side of the cafeteria with the other jocks and cheerleaders. Then there's Kyle Bonagan. He lives by the water, too, only it's called Dent Creek, past the railroad tracks on the eastern side of town. He's a Tracker and sits on the left-hand side of the cafeteria with other students who are on the debate team or play in the band. Faith Mason wears black every day—black boots laced all the way up to her knees, black tights, black skirt, black tank top, black jacket. She wears thick black eyeliner, black lipstick and nails and has a gazillion piercings starting in the center of her lower lip. Of course, she sits by the fruit juice machine.

Then there's another table, right by the exit doors. A group of guys sit there. I don't know where they live but they're wearing all the latest hip-hop gear: oversize shirts, baggy jeans, boots—brown or black—and they always wear flashy watches or chains. They aren't really called anything and the other students keep their distance from them. I don't know if it's just their clothes—which would be mad stupid—or the fact that a couple of the guys are known for their bad attitudes and willingness to beat down anybody that even looks at them sideways.

Me, I live midway between the Richies and the no-names, those are the people who are considered middle class. We don't have too much money but we have enough. I don't dress like a goth or a geek but I'm definitely not a part of the hip-hop crowd either. So I sit at one of the center tables, which sometimes makes me feel like I'm on display. Usually I just pull out my bag lunch, slip my earbuds in and listen to my iPod for the forty-five minutes that's our only designated downtime.

So that's what I'm doing today when my usually quiet table consisting of maybe one or two other no-names is invaded. I've already ignored my sandwich and only have my butterscotch crumpet and half a Sprite left from my lunch. I had pulled out the small sketchbook I carry around with me religiously but I hadn't bothered to open it up yet. Ne-Yo is blasting from my iPod when I look up and notice who's sitting across from me: Sasha Carrington—a Richie—and her faithful sidekick, Jake Kramer—a Tracker.

In the months that I'd been at Settlemans, this was by far one of the weirdest hookups I'd seen. Sasha is Latina or something, I think, despite the Anglo surname. Her hair is dark with golden highlights. Her skin is this olive color that reminds me of people I see on television who come from, like, Greece or the Mediterranean or someplace like that. She always dresses nicely, mostly in designer clothes, and carries a huge designer bag and wears makeup. Jake, on the other hand, has a shaggy kind of look. He's pale, with dark brown hair that always looks like it needs to be cut. Today is no different—with big curly locks falling low on his forehead, almost brushing his shoulder. A Richie and a Tracker—I wonder if they are a couple, like, boyfriend and girlfriend.

"Hi," Sasha says with her easy smile that makes her cheeks more prominent.

I lift a hand to wave, not wanting to give the impression that I'm happy to see them sitting there.

Jake waves back, the right corner of his mouth lifting in a shy smile.

"Whatcha listenin' to?" Sasha asks.

I don't really hear her. I'm just sort of reading her lips because my music is loud.

"Ne-Yo."

Sasha nods. "'So Sick of Love Songs?'"

I shake my head. "No. 'Miss Independent.'"

"Oooh, the Jamie Foxx remix?" Jake asks.

I nod.

"Wanna go outside?"

"No," I quickly reply.

"It's loud in here," Jake says.

I shrug. I was fine before they came. If it's too loud for them, they can go outside.

They're both quiet for a few minutes then Sasha stands and comes around the table. My hair is up in a ponytail as usual. Still I'm shocked when she taps the back of my neck and says, "Cool tat."

Frowning, I realize she's referring to the birthmark on the back of my neck. It kind of looks like a cursive *M*. I know this because I've looked in the mirror to see it a time or two. And I guess since I always wear my hair up, other people can see it, as well.

"It's my birthmark," I say, pulling away from her. It's creepy the way she touches me, her fingers rubbing over the mark. I feel this weird stirring in the pit of my stomach, kind of like I need to throw up and then not.

Sasha and Jake look at each other then back to me. "We should go outside," she says. "To talk."

I'm confused. Why all of a sudden does Sasha, the Richie, want to talk to me? It doesn't matter. I don't want to talk to her.

Just as I open my mouth to say something, the bell rings. I yank my earbuds out and shrug again. "Too late. Gotta get to class."

I scoop up my book bag, purse and trash and stand up to leave. Jake stands, too, coming around to the side of the table where I am.

"We can talk after school. Sasha's got a car. She only has her learner's permit so she has to have a driver. But he lets her drive sometimes so she can take us both home."

Sasha rolls her eyes at Jake. I don't really blame her. That was way too much information.

Then I'm, like, what is this—some kind of threesome? I saw it one time on the X-rated channel my father had on his satellite television. Now I really feel like puking.

I can feel my forehead scrunching up in a frown. "No thanks," I say, turning away from him.

"Krystal."

I hear Sasha calling my name as I try to keep walking. Other kids either eager to get to class or just tired of the noise of the cafeteria bump into me on their way out. She calls my name again and I stop, reluctantly, that funny feeling in my stomach rising again. I turn and Sasha and Jake are still standing in the same spot where I left them at the table.

"We need to talk," Sasha says, all serious-looking.

"Whatever," I say and keep moving. Those two are weird. Weirder than me, I guess. So I vow to steer clear of them. I've got enough troubles.

Apparently the plan is for my troubles to just keep on piling up today. World History is my last class of the day. And while I usually kind of enjoy learning about different cultures and all the events that have brought us to this point, today I'm just not feeling it.

It isn't really the class. Mrs. Tremble is sitting behind her desk as usual, thin silver-rimmed glasses hanging on the bulbous tip of her nose, reading her lesson plan verbatim. That's either because she is too old—really, she's, like, in her eighties—or too round to stand up like the other teachers and write on the chalkboard.

The desks are in a double *U* shape with everyone whose

last name starts with a letter from the beginning of the alphabet in the inner *U* and the end of the alphabet in the outer semicircle. That puts Alyssa Turner right behind me. Her sidekick, Camy Sherwood, is sitting right beside her.

Midway through the lesson on the Egyptian pyramids, I feel a little jolt and realize it's somebody kicking my chair. I turn around to see Alyssa with her goddess black braids and eyeliner-etched eyes staring at me with a smirk on her face. Camy's giggling. Her smile, which is lined with braces, catches the rays of the sun peeking through the windows, nearly blinding me.

"Hey, new girl," Alyssa says.

I roll my eyes and turn back around. She kicks my chair again.

"Not funny," I whisper over my shoulder.

"Yeah, you talking to Franklin's definitely a joke. What makes you think you can just waltz into town and start taking our guys?"

Was she serious? I mean, come on, the boy's been following me around for weeks, looking at me and trying to talk to me. While *I* have been minding my own business.

On the other hand, is she serious with that "taking our guys" comment? If I wanted to talk to a guy, which I do not, I could talk to whatever guy I wanted.

"When I was in elementary school my mother used to label everything that belonged to me. As far as I could tell, Franklin didn't have a name tag on."

Now I can't tell if it's my words—which I actually think are quite clever—or the fact that I had the nerve to respond at all that has Camy looking from me to Alyssa like her eyes are about to pop out of her head. Alyssa's definitely a Richie; she's head of the cheerleading squad and would probably be voted "Biggest Bitch" in the yearbook. Camy was like a puppet with Alyssa pulling her strings.

"I don't need to mark my territory. I'm not an animal," Alyssa quips.

Okay, she can apparently give as good as she gets. Un-fortunately, I don't even care enough to go another round with her. "Look, we talked. He walked me to my locker. End of story. Nobody's poaching on your territory."

"Just make sure you don't, new girl."

The clapping of Mrs. Tremble's ruler against her desk delays my response, which is cool because out of the corner of my eye I spot something, or should I say someone, else. Someone who definitely should not be in World History class or any other class for that matter.

Sitting on top of the file cabinet, way in the back of the room, wearing the same clothes I saw him in last night, is Ricky. Okay, well, I guess spirits don't have a change of clothes, so they spend eternity wearing the same outfit they died in. Gross.

His arms are crossed over his chest and he's looking down at me, of course. But then his gaze kind of shifts behind me to Alyssa and Camy. I wonder what he's thinking.

No. I don't.

I don't care what he's thinking or why he's here. I don't want to see him or talk to him. Or do I? I can't help but notice again how cute he is.

Mrs. Tremble's voice drones on and on until finally, thankfully, the bell rings. I wasn't taking any notes so grabbing my stuff only takes half a second. I'm turning, pushing my chair back and about to exit the row when Alyssa reaches out and forcefully grabs my elbow.

"Look, don't think because I let you slide once I'll do it again. Know your place and stay in it."

I pull out of her grasp. "Get out of my face," I say, giving her a look that I hope says I'm not playing. Because I'm not. There's no way I'm going to fight over a boy, especially one I'm not even interested in. But I have no intention of letting her bully me either.

I am already walking away when I hear her screeching something about "new girl," then her voice sounds funny and she screams. Turning back, I see her just as her feet flip from under her and she hurls face-first to the floor.

"Ohmigod, Alyssa! Are you all right?" Camy is right there, dropping her books and falling to her knees to help Alyssa, who is looking up, her eyes shooting daggers at me.

As for me, I ignore the daggers and resist the urge to laugh at her fall. Why? Because I'm more stunned at the fact that Ricky's standing right next to where Alyssa was a few seconds ago. His arms aren't folded over his chest anymore. Instead his head is thrown back as he laughs. Nobody can hear the sound but me, just like nobody in that room knows he's probably the one who pushed Alyssa.

Great, now my ghost friend is fighting my battles.

five

I slam the door to my bedroom shut, not sure why I'm mad, just knowing that I want desperately to be alone.

I get that feeling a lot—the wanting to be alone. It's Friday, so I toss my books into a corner vowing not to touch them again until late Sunday night.

Kicking my shoes off, I move toward my bed. Not because I'm sleepy but because I want to get off my feet. Lazy-teenager syndrome, Grandma Bentley calls it. I talked to her last week. She asked me to come to South Carolina to spend the summer with her. I didn't answer because I don't really want to go down South where heat waves suffocate the air twenty-four hours a day and the most exciting thing is riding to the Piggly Wiggly for a frozen fruit bar. Compared to that, Lincoln seems like a resort in the Bahamas.

My thoughts of summer are interrupted by what I see on my bed. Right in the center of my puffy blue comforter is a sketch pad, charcoal tip pencils, markers and paints.

Had Janet been reading my mind? Maybe she has some freaky power, too. How had she known I'd been thinking of drawing, something that once had seemed to be all I could think of? For a second my fingers tingle as I see the art supplies. I want to touch them, to pick them up and lose myself in my sketches.

No. That was in my other life. The one where I was a normal—well, somewhat normal—teenager and all was well.

All is definitely not well now, I say to myself as I use my arm to push the contents off my bed, ignoring the sound as they scatter on the floor so that I can lie down.

I roll to my side, pulling my knees up to my chest, cradling my head on my folded arm and sigh.

This is my life now. This is all I do.

Go to school.

Come home.

Sleep.

Think.

You really need to get a life.

I jump at the sound of his voice but don't bother to turn to look at him before saying, "That's cute coming from someone who's dead."

He laughs and the butterflies in my stomach flutter. *You didn't like the gift your mother bought you?*

"How can you tell?"

Well, it was rude to throw it on the floor no matter how you felt about it.

"I didn't ask for your opinion."

But I gave it to you anyway. You know how many kids would kill for their parents to do something nice for them— to give them something—anything at all?

I did know and I felt like a heel. But I wasn't about to tell him that. "What do you want, Ricky?"

We covered that yesterday.

"I'm not a cop. I don't know how you expect me to help you."

You can start by getting out of bed. It's not even five o'clock and you act like you're in for the night.

"That's because I am."

That's crazy. If I could, do you know what I'd be doing right now?

I don't know but I'm sure he's going to tell me. Just a small part of me is curious. Who was Ricky Watson? Before he died, I mean. Who were his friends? What did he do in his spare time? Did he have a girlfriend?

That last question comes out of nowhere and I feel my cheeks flush. Glad I didn't say it aloud.

It's Friday so I'd probably shoot some hoops after school till around seven or eight. Then I'd run home, catch a shower and change, hit the streets for the night.

"Hit the streets? And do what?"

He shrugs. *Maybe go to a club or catch a new movie. Or if I have a hottie on hand, I'd hook up with her.*

My heart plunges, taking a fall so steep I almost lose my breath. A "hottie"? He'd be with a "hottie." I shake my head, waving my hand in his direction. What do I care if he's with a "hottie" or not?

"TMI. TMI."

He chuckles. *No, that's not too much information. I didn't say what I'd do with the hottie when I hooked up with her.*

I turn my head away because instantly looking at him is making my chest hurt more. Why is that? I just met him. It's not like we're having some grand love affair. Not like he's my first love. I've never even had a boyfriend. I've never been kissed—French or American. Then again, all this is nonsense, he's some kind of poltergeist, remember?

Look at you blushing, he teases. *I'll bet you've never even kissed a boy, have you, Krystal?*

I jump up off the bed, wondering if his kind can read minds. "Now that is definitely TMI!"

He shrugs. *You can tell me. I mean, who am I going to tell if you did? Did you let him get more than a kiss?*

I stalk across the room, my back to him, my head starting to ache slightly at the nerve he has to talk to me like this. Or is it the truth in those words that has my heart pounding?

The truth shall set you free, I hear echoing from a distance in my head.

"Look, I don't care what you would have been doing if you hadn't been shot up! All I know is you're here now and it's pissing me off."

He is quiet. So quiet that I might have thought he'd left but I can still feel him. It is funny how this spirit communication works. Then again, I've never really opened myself up to this troublesome quirk I seem to have. So I really have nothing to compare this incident with. And nobody to ask about it.

Isn't that the story of my life?

Questions. Issues. Problems to solve. But nobody to talk to, nobody to give me advice or help me find the answers. Sometimes life just sucks.

If you turn on your computer I can show you when I died and what they said about me.

"I don't care," I say quickly. Too quickly and it sounds really rude.

I need you to care, Krystal. You're the only one who can help me.

"Why?" I whirl around then, so fast I almost fall onto the floor. But I'm standing near my desk so I grab hold of the end to keep myself upright. "You're the ghost. Why can't you just fly around or vanish and reappear or whatever you do and haunt the people who did this to you? Make them tell the truth or something."

It doesn't work that way.

"Then what way does it work?" My voice grows higher and I know I need to calm down before Janet comes upstairs. She's in the den, where she always is, either reading a book or staring out the window like the answer to her problems is out there. I guess we're searching for the same thing, mother and daughter. We need answers. Or do we need help? Maybe we need both.

I don't really know, he says and moves closer to me. So close that I think I smell cologne. Something sweet but still like it's made for a boy.

I turn my head away from him.

You won't be able to run from me. I do know that.

I look back at him feeling the anger bubbling inside me. "Why? Why won't you leave me alone? I shouldn't have to help you if I don't want to."

You shouldn't. But I think it's your job or, like, your purpose.

Just as I'm about to tell him I don't have a job, as evidenced by my lack of money, and that I've never had a purpose besides being Janet and Calvin's daughter, I hear footsteps on the stairs.

My room is at the very top of the first landing of stairs. If the footsteps keep going then I'm safe. That means whoever it is will probably go down the long hallway into another room or keep going up the next flight of stairs to the exercise room.

The footsteps stop.

No such luck for me.

There's a brisk knock at my door.

"Krystal. We're going out to dinner tonight. Be downstairs in fifteen minutes."

Gerald's voice is deep, dripping with authority. My dad never spoke to me in that tone. I hate it when Gerald does. So I don't say anything.

Ricky is still standing close, staring at me with a funny look on his face.

"Krystal? Did you hear me? I know you're not asleep

because I just heard you talking. Get off the cell phone and let's go."

He knocks on the door one more time then I hear him turning the knob. I move quickly, lifting a foot to stomp over the middle of my bed to get to the door before he has a chance to come inside. I don't want him to see there's a boy in my room.

Just as the door swings open I'm right on the other side, looking up into eyes darker than the night sky, a head full of thick black hair, gray at the temples. His mustache is thick, too, totally covering his top lip. He's looking at me sternly with one hand on the doorknob and the other straddling the top part of the door.

I can't stand him. From the first day Janet brought him to our little apartment I knew I'd never like him. His beady little eyes spelled "fake wannabe" clearly. I don't know why Janet couldn't see it. Maybe she didn't want to. I guess that means I *did* want to see it, like maybe I just wasn't going to like any man with Janet besides my dad. Doesn't matter—I don't like him and he seems to like me even less.

"Fifteen minutes," he says when he sees me.

I nod. I don't talk to him any more than I talk to Janet. Neither one of them is on my favorite person list right now. Gerald's actually at the very bottom of the list.

"You're not a mute. Answer me when I speak to you."

I'm not a mute but I'm definitely tired of him bossing me around. He is *not* my father.

"Krystal," he says in a warning tone.

"I heard you," I finally say through clenched teeth.

He frowns. I think he wants to say something else, probably something really rude and mean to me, but he doesn't.

"Fifteen minutes," is all he mutters.

I push the door until it slams again, then turn and press my back against it. For a minute I close my eyes and when

I open them again it's to see Ricky standing right in front of me.

You handled that well.

He's being sarcastic and I'm definitely not in the mood. "Mind your own business," I snap.

Maybe you just need to loosen up, stop being so defensive all the time. Not everybody's out to get you.

"I don't think they are," I lie. That's exactly what I think. Or rather, I think everybody has an ulterior motive, which usually takes them out of my life. So if I'm meant to be alone then why not just start out with that goal? Why even bother taking a chance?

I'm just about to say that but in the next second he's moving closer to me like the men do in movies. His head's kind of tilted as he approaches, his eyes not really looking at mine. I think he's looking at my mouth. Like he's going to kiss me. But that's not possible. He can't kiss me.

I've never been kissed.

Still, I think I might like it…if Ricky is my first.

SIX

There are two hotels in Lincoln—one that only rich people can afford to stay in and one that normal people like me and my father can afford to stay in.

Tonight we're eating at Solange. It's the ritzy restaurant with food I can't pronounce let alone eat on the menu. It's located on the lobby floor of the Nokland Hotel—the one that rich people can afford.

I guess this is what's meant by marrying up. In that case, Janet did well for herself. My father draws a comic strip that appears in lots of different newspapers, including the *New York Daily News*. That wasn't glamorous to Janet, but to me, I thought it was like having my own personal celebrity. Janet always said my father needed to grow up.

So a month ago she married Gerald. He moved us out of the apartment we were renting down by the lake and into a four-bedroom, three-bath house that looked more like a bed-and-breakfast than a home. He told Janet she didn't need to work, which I think Janet really liked. In New York she worked at Macy's doing makeup at the Clinique counter. That's all she said she could do since she never graduated from college. A fact I sometimes felt she was trying to blame on me. But I don't even know how she'd fix her mouth to say that was my fault. I didn't ask to be born and I'm sure my father didn't force her to have sex. Maybe she should have taken the advice she always gave me about unprotected sex.

Maybe those thoughts are rude or out of line. But they're my thoughts so nobody can censor them.

Anyway, we're at the restaurant and Gerald is walking with his shoulders back and his nose tilted high, like if he lowers it he might smell something he doesn't like. Janet's right behind him and I'm behind her. They sit and I follow. They pick up their menus and I stare straight ahead, out the window that stretches over the whole wall on the other side of the room.

It's dark outside; we didn't leave in fifteen minutes as Gerald had originally said. Instead we'd had to wait for Janet to change into "something more suitable for going out." She really has changed since moving to this small town and hooking up with this big idiot. She'd had on jeans, a blouse and nice open-toed shoes. She looked fine to me. There was really no need for her to change. But Gerald is pleased that she did because the long cream-colored skirt and peach blouse she is wearing goes a lot better with his beige suit and burnt orange tie. It is all about "the look" with them now.

I still have on the jeans I'd worn to school and a T-shirt. Gerald had frowned at me and was about to say something when I saw Janet put a hand on his arm and shake her head. The movement said I was a lost cause.

She is probably right.

"Look, Krys, they have chicken on the menu," Janet says all bright and smiley. She's happy to be here, probably happy that all three of us are out looking like a real family.

I try not to be so sulky by sitting up in the chair and picking up the menu. But as I read, the gloom of my normal mood returns and I see the chicken she's referring to is a chicken tender meal in the lower corner of the menu titled "Kids' Meals."

So now I'm a "kid"? A fifteen-year-old, five-foot-four, with every bit of an A cup breasts, kid. I drop the menu as if it were burning my fingers. "I don't like chicken fingers."

"Well, I know how much you like fried chicken so I figured this would be the same."

Janet rarely eats meat; that's probably why she thinks fried chicken and processed chicken tenders are the same thing.

"Not," I say solemnly.

"Then order something else," Gerald says quickly. Sternly. I'm getting on his nerves, like I always do.

That's just fine because he gets on my nerves, too. If Janet hadn't married him maybe she'd get back with my dad. Speaking of which, I push my chair back and get ready to stand.

"Where are you going?" Janet asks before I can make my getaway.

"Bathroom," I lie quickly.

"The proper way is to ask to be excused. You're old enough that by now you should be using better manners."

My eyes cut fast to Gerald. There are so many words rolling through my head that I'd like to say to him. But—unlike what he thinks—I do have manners. I'm not about to cuss out my mother's new husband, not in a crowded restaurant at least.

"I need to be excused to go to the restroom. Do you want to risk not giving me permission, Gerald?" My lips squeeze tightly together after I speak. That's the only way I can hold in the rest of what I want to say.

"Mr. Gerald," he reminds me that this is what he'd like to be called.

I smile sweetly and as phony as Clay Aiken when he first denied being gay. "Mr. Gerald."

"Go ahead. Your mother will order something for you. Something much healthier than fried chicken or chicken fingers or whatever the two of you were discussing."

My eyes close to tiny slits. I know because my vision is sliced thin. I'm so mad I want to swing on him. Yes, I want to hit my stepfather. I'm sure there are millions of other teens in the world who can relate to that feeling. Unfortunately, none of them are standing here with me to offer moral support, so Janet stands, putting a hand on my arm.

"Are you okay, baby? Do you need me to go with you?"

"What?" I frown at her. "No. I don't need an escort. I'm fine."

"Would you like me to order for you?" Janet asks, although Gerald has already spoken.

I've already turned to leave and wave my hand back in her direction. "Fine. Whatever."

I should have stayed home, in my room, by myself. This is too much, too soon. I don't want to be out with them like we are a happy family. Because we aren't. I'm definitely not. I hate living in Lincoln. I hate that my parents are divorced and with every passing day I hate Gerald.

While I'm walking checking off my mental list of things I hate about my life I'm reaching into my pocket for my phone. With one hand I hit the buttons that will dial my father's house. I put the phone to my ear, waiting for him to answer, hoping he'll pick up and that the answer to my next question will be yes.

Instead I hear, "You've reached Calvin Bentley. I'm not available to take your call right now, so leave your name, number and a brief message and I'll get back to you. Peace."

Peace?

Since when does Daddy say that? Doesn't matter, there's definitely no peace in my life.

"Hey, Daddy, it's me, Krystal," I speak into the phone

after it beeps for me to leave a message. I don't know why I'm telling him who I am. He only has one daughter. "Um, can you call me back as soon as you get this message? It's really important." I say goodbye and flip the phone shut, then head toward the bathroom.

I figure I'd better make it look good. Knowing Gerald, he'd probably followed me out here. But just as I'm about to go in the bathroom door I hear voices to my right.

The restaurant is on an angle, at the end of a long hallway coming from the lobby of the hotel. The restrooms are along the right side at the end of the hall. There's a *T* shape at the end so I can either go left or right. Left will lead me into the bathrooms, right will lead down a smaller hall and to the door marked Exit.

That's where the voices are coming from.

Did you tell her everything? This is a female voice, the one that first stopped me.

I figure it's none of my business and I move to make the left turn when the next voice halts my steps.

No. Not yet. She needs time to get used to the idea first. Ricky?

Now I know I haven't been talking to this guy—no, this ghost—for long. One day to be precise. So I shouldn't just know his voice even without seeing him. But I do. I think I even hear it in my sleep.

I'm walking toward that exit door even though my mind is screaming this is a bad idea.

What's there to get used to? If she can hear you, she can help us.

Help us? Did this chick just say "us"?

Anger and curiosity brewing together isn't such a good mix. So when the flat of my hand pushes the door open, the shocked look on their faces could only have mirrored the one on mine.

There they are, near the steps. Ricky in his jeans and

T-shirt and some girl—some girl ghost, as evidenced by her transparent appearance—with short curly hair and wearing way too much makeup.

They both stare at me as I stare at them, a standoff like they have on TV when the dead body is found and the wife's standing over him with blood on her hands.

Krystal? Ricky speaks first.

"Who is she?" I speak next.

Trina.

His girlfriend.

They both speak together.

seven

I am out of that hallway so fast a breeze probably formed behind me. I can still hear Ricky calling my name but I can't see him.

Tears are stinging my eyes so seeing isn't a high probability. Why I am about to cry I don't know. Ricky's not my boyfriend so I shouldn't care if he has a girlfriend. My feelings shouldn't be hurt. I shouldn't feel betrayed. But I do. Again.

I make it back to the table and Janet is immediately up and at my side. I lift a hand, halting her steps. "I'm fine. Just tired. Can we hurry up and eat so I can go home?"

On the one side of me, still-sitting Gerald is frowning. On the other side, Janet's expression goes from worried to saddened and I feel a pinch of guilt, knowing that it's my fault.

Right about now I don't even care.

I'm too busy wondering if I got played by a ghost.

Even the thought is stupid and I shiver as I think it. What's wrong with me? Why do I even hear or see these spirits? This is so crazy I can't believe it, let alone expect anybody else to believe it. So even though I know Janet wants to know what's wrong with me, I can never tell her.

Not that I desperately want her and Daddy to get back together and definitely not that I think I'm losing my mind because I see dead people.

I manage to get through dinner without crying and/or throwing up. The more I think about the fact that I was actually jealous at seeing two ghosts together, the more I feel sick. Maybe I need to be medicated or, worse, sent to a mental institution.

Those thoughts run through my mind as I also worry over the fact that Daddy hasn't returned my call. I haven't talked to him in a couple of weeks. Where is he?

The air is humid and thick. It's nighttime so it should be cooler. Just yesterday it was so chilly I almost put on a jacket. The weather here is so strange.

I climb the stairs and go to my room the moment we get back from dinner, but then I don't want to stay in my room. I am afraid Ricky will come back.

So when Gerald and Janet are closed in their bedroom probably doing things that would make me want to gouge my eyes out, I sneak downstairs and out the back door to sit on the patio.

Our house faces some trees and just past the trees is a small beach, then endless water. In the distance I hear the waves. Closing my eyes, I try to concentrate on the soothing sounds and for a minute or so it works.

Then there's moaning, like someone's in pain. It's my plan to ignore the moan because for some reason I think it's not really happening.

Denial at its best.

Unfortunately, it persists and my eyes creep open. Silent prayers are going up to the heavens that I'm still alone out here. Opening my eyes all the way, I sigh. Prayer works.

Or maybe not.

The sound is getting louder, turning into maybe a cry. I sit up in the chair and decide I'm just going to the end of our yard to see what's going on. My wobbly legs take me a little farther until I'm standing on the beach.

The water looks dark, like a shiny piece of black material. There's no moon out and no stars. A few minutes ago—back on the patio—I was hot. Now I fold my arms over my chest and fight against chattering teeth.

The cry echoes in the air from behind me. I turn quickly, see the tall woman in the long white gown and fall flat on my butt.

Help me, she says, reaching her hands out to me. My gaze follows the length of her arms to the tight bodice of her gown, up her neck and to her face—to her half face. The other half is completely rotted. The scream that ripples through me should have been loud and eardrum shattering but just then a huge wave comes rolling in. From the corner of my eye I see it building and know that when it comes crashing down it will take me with it. So I roll in the sand, get to my knees then struggle to stand. Breaking into a run, I refuse to look back. Heading straight for the house, I go upstairs to my room where I close and lock my door.

My chest's heaving as I sit on the floor trying to catch my breath. I wonder if a lock and a fear as big as the continent would keep that woman and any other ghosts away.

Oh, God, I hope so.

Sleep hadn't come easy but it finally came and I didn't dream, thank goodness. I don't think I could have handled another traumatic experience like a nightmare.

It's Sunday and I know Janet isn't going to church. She hasn't been since we left New York, which also means I haven't been either. Grandma Bentley would have a heart attack if she knew that.

Hey, maybe that's what I needed—Jesus or an exorcism.

You need to get up out of this bed. It's almost noon.

I jump at the sound of his voice, immediately pulling the covers up to my chest.

"Get out!" I yell, not loud enough for anybody to come running to my room full of questions. But at just the right tone so he can tell I'm serious.

Calm down. You're all uptight first thing on a Sunday morning.

"Uptight!" I say, sitting up in my bed, forgetting all about the sheets until I see his gaze drop down.

I don't have big breasts but they're still there and they're just barely covered by a thin tank top. I pull the sheet up again and tuck it under my armpits. "Listen, I don't know what type of game you're playing but I'm not in the mood. In fact, I think you and your *girlfriend* need to find somebody else to help you."

He laughs but I don't see what's so funny.

"Just get out of my room. Out of my life." I sigh heavily then fall back onto my pillows. "Isn't my life bad enough without dead people waltzing into it?"

Why do you think your life is so bad? From where I'm standing, you've got it all. A great house near the water, almost near the Richies. You have your mother and your stepdad living with you, taking you out to dinner and all that wholesome family stuff. What could you possibly have to complain about?

I turn my head toward the sound of his voice. He's standing to the right of my bed, in front of the nightstand with my clock radio and lamp.

"You have no idea what my life is really like. All this," I say, waving my arm toward everything in the room, "is like a stage, set up for the performance of a lifetime. But happily ever after isn't in my future. I'm definitely no Cinderella."

You got that right. Cinderella would have been up by now scrubbing those floors.

He's laughing harder now and I can't help but crack a smile. That dimple in his cheek is just too cute.

Still, he says, trying to stop laughing, *it can't be that bad.*

"It is."

Tell me about it.

I shake my head. "That's not why you're here."

No, but maybe we can make a trade. You help me. I help you.

"How can a spirit help me with my life?"

I won't know until you tell me what's so wrong with your life.

He has a point there so I sit up again, resting my back against the headboard. I could probably tell him what is going on in my life that has me so pissed off and depressed at the same time. Who is he going to tell if he's dead?

"Nobody else can see you, can they?" I ask as we stop walking through the park. We're far away from the swings and monkey bars where there are a few little kids with their parents playing. Down two slopes and off the path that the speed walkers or runners take, I sit on the ground and stare out across the jutting rocks and slow trickle of water.

Unless they have the same power that you do, no.

I sigh heavily because I don't even know what power I have. Nor do I want it.

How long have you been doing this?

"Doing what?"

This. The whole ghost whisperer thing.

I hate the way that sounds. Like that show that comes on television with the woman who can talk to ghosts and helps them with some unresolved problem. That's fiction, entertainment. This is my life.

I just shrug instead of answering him.

Don't like it much, huh?

"How'd you guess?"

Why don't you like it? Man, if I could have a cool super-power I'd love it. You know the things I could have done if I was powerful?

"What? Like stay alive?"

He chuckles but then looks at me more seriously. *You know, you could make a person feel just as crappy as you without even trying.*

I shrug again.

Like I said, your life can't be that bad. Probably just some spoiled brat complaining while the rest of us sit back and want what you have.

My neck almost snaps I turn my head in his direction so fast. He's sitting right beside me, his knees drawn up in front of him, his arms wrapped around them. "I told you, you know nothing about my life. If you did, you'd know the last thing anybody could call me is spoiled."

Then let's try ungrateful.

I move to stand up. "No. Let's try I'm outta here. Help yourself with your afterlife problems, dead boy."

But before I can stalk away after my perfect exit line I'm falling to the ground, my hands coming up flat to keep my face from meeting the grass. I roll over quickly, wondering if he'd touched me. No, he couldn't have touched me. Not for real, I don't think.

Ricky's still laughing, something I figure must have been one of his favorite pastimes. He hasn't moved from his position.

"You're an idiot," I say, scrambling up once more.

And you're clumsy. You didn't see that big rock right there?

I'm on my knees now and as he points I follow his arm. Sure enough, there's a rock, similar to the ones in the creek, halfway buried beneath the grass. So, no, he hadn't pushed me, but he'd gotten a good enough laugh at me falling on my face.

The reasons why not to like Ricky were quickly adding up. 1) He's not a real boy, just a spirit. 2) He has a girlfriend. Her name is Trina. 3) He thinks he knows everything. 4) He has a sick sense of humor.

Come on back over here and sit down. If somebody comes up the path you're going to look like some psycho talking to yourself.

He probably has a point. I am sitting sideways so it would be easy for someone coming by to see and/or hear me talking to the air.

I huff and reluctantly do as he says. "I must be psycho for sitting here talking to you," I can't resist saying.

Man, this is so jacked. Of all the ghost whisperers in the world, I end up with you.

"Feel free to go, Ricky. I was doing just fine before you showed up!"

No, you weren't. You're running around looking like somebody just stole your bike day in and day out. You treat your mother like crap and don't give her husband much more respect. And you stay in that room like it's some sort of hideout.

Well, tell me how you really feel. I feel like saying this to him, but I'm not ready to admit that his assessment of me and my life is dangerously close to the truth, as usual.

"Who cares what you think," I say and look the other way. I don't care what he thinks. He's not that important to me to care.

Hey, you don't have to care what I think. But you're too cute to be holed up in that house all the time. And you're too young for all this drama.

Could he read my mind...and did he just say I was cute? Okay, my head is slowly turning back in his direction and I squint my eyes when I look at him. "Don't try to flirt with me. You have a girlfriend, remember." Thinking of the other ghost makes my head hurt.

And there is that smile again. He doesn't chuckle this time but his dark skin seems to highlight his superwhite teeth. He lifts a hand and rubs his fingers over his chin. The sun catches on his watch and there is a silver glare that almost has me closing my eyes. *I'll admit, if circumstances were different I might definitely try to holla at you. But your foul attitude would probably turn me off.*

Did I have a foul attitude?

"Whatever."

Were you like this where you used to live or did you just get this new personality when you came to Lincoln?

"How'd you know I just moved here?" He'd only started stalking me in the past week or so.

Because I've lived here all my life and I don't remember you.

"Maybe I stayed off your radar. I don't normally hang with gang members."

See that's the New York in you talking. This is Lincoln, small town, small population. So if a group of guys start hanging out together we're more like a clique or a crew, which sound better to me than a "gang."

"Wait, you're talking about the guys that sit near the doors in the cafeteria. The ones who all wear the same black-and-red hat?"

Yeah. He nods. *That's them.*

"They like to get into trouble," I say, relaying the rumors I've heard.

Yeah, they can be a pretty rebellious bunch.

"Then why hang out with them?"

He looks at me funny, then quirks one thick eyebrow upward. I can't help but smile.

It's a long story. But mostly it was because of my brother.

"Your brother Antoine?"

We call him Twan. And, yeah, he's still runnin' with the crew.

Ricky doesn't look too pleased with that idea. "Even after your death he's still with them? That's stupid."

You don't know them. It's not that easy to walk away once you're in. Besides, where else would he go if he does get out?

"Is that why they killed you, because you wanted to get out?" It sounds too serious to me. Killing somebody because they didn't want to hang with you anymore?

They didn't kill me, he says solemnly.

"So who did?"

That's what I want you to find out.

eight

SO last night instead of seeing more spirits or dreaming of being in the graveyard with more dead people, I dreamt of Ricky. In the real sense, I mean. He was living and breathing and he was my boyfriend. We were sitting by the creek in the park, just like we had yesterday. He held my hand, touched my cheek, then he kissed me.

It is at that point I wake up. My body is hot all over, even though I'd long since kicked the covers off me. My hand instantly goes to my lips as I remember the kiss in my dream. Then I remember Ricky was also in my dream, alive. Which is damn simple of me since I know for a fact that Ricky is dead.

So I still haven't been kissed and I'm crushing on a dead boy.

No way, no how.

As I head for school I'm determined to keep Ricky Watson out of sight and definitely out of mind. If I'm craving a kiss, or a boyfriend for that matter, I'd just as soon find somebody with a change of clothes…and a pulse.

"I called you yesterday," Franklin says, coming up beside me with a smile that I admit is cute but kind of silly.

No way is anybody that happy all the time. I just

slammed my locker door shut and there he was, appearing as if by magic or fate.

"My battery was dead," I say automatically, not real sure why I am lying.

He nods as if he believes me. Today he's wearing jeans, dark blue, that are too long and rest on his white shellhead sneakers. His shirt is polo, sky blue, the horse on his left side is yellow. He smells good. Probably using some of his father's cologne because he smells older, like a boy trying to be a man.

"I'll walk you to class," he says. I'm just about to tell him it's not necessary when over Franklin's right shoulder I see Ricky.

For a second I'm alarmed, then I remember nobody else can see him. Unless they also have some freaky afterlife power. He's leaning against the locker, directly behind Franklin. He's frowning, looking Franklin up and down like he doesn't approve.

This, of course, ticks me off. Who does he think he is? I don't need his approval to be with Franklin. As a matter of fact, the thought of being with Franklin makes a lot more sense then being with a ghost.

"Ah, sure," I say, trying to get Franklin away from Ricky.

But as I speak Franklin follows my gaze, turning to see what I'm looking at. At first I'm worried but, of course, he sees nothing and when he turns back to me he looks puzzled.

"You okay, Krystal?"

"Huh?" I know I sound confused so I make myself stop looking at Ricky, who is now using his fingers to thrust into his mouth like he's gagging. "I'm fine. Just thought I saw…ah, a bug or something."

Franklin nods. "Well, you know the town's close to the water and all this rain we've been getting lately draws a lot of insects. My father says we might be heading for a hurricane or another big storm."

We're walking toward my class now, Ricky having been left behind. But Franklin's mention of a hurricane catches my attention. "It's April, Franklin. Hurricane season doesn't start until June."

Franklin shakes his head. "Not in Lincoln. We've been known to have weird weather patterns. Like El Niño just picks on us for the hell of it."

"El Niño?"

"Yeah, it's the name they gave the wacky weather pattern that warms the central and eastern Tropical Pacific waters. Causes all sorts of storms and weather anomalies."

I stop walking because I'm at the door to Biology now. "And what are you, the town meteorologist?"

He laughs, then reaches out a hand and touches my hair. The touch is light but it moves him a lot closer to me. My heartbeat falters a bit but I blink quickly and it goes away.

"Nah, that's my father. I'm just really interested in things that aren't normal. I like to find oddities and see what makes them tick."

Well, he'd picked a great oddity in me. I try to smile and move out of his grasp at the same time, with finesse so he doesn't notice that I'm uncomfortable with him touching me.

"Can I sit with you at lunch?" he asks.

"No," I hurry up and answer, remembering my lunch intrusion on Friday. "Are you even on my lunch period?"

Franklin shakes his head, still smiling. "Yeah, I am. Do you want to sit with me instead?"

I open my mouth, almost asking him which side he sat on, but we're interrupted.

"Hey, Franklin," Sasha says in a cheery tone as she comes up to stand next to us. She's wearing a long crinkly skirt that starts out this dark shade of teal at the bottom and gets lighter heading to the top. Her blouse is white and cinched around her tiny waist with a thick gold belt that matches her earrings and her shoes.

I try not to envy how cute and stylish she looks, seemingly without even trying, when she says, "Hi, Krystal."

It is way too early in the morning for all this cheerfulness. "Hey," I mumble as I hear Franklin speak to her, too.

The bell rings and everybody looks up above the door where one of the speakers rests. We stare at it for a few seconds, as if our looks alone will shut it up.

"I should go," I say, recovering first.

Franklin takes a step back, adjusting his books in his arm. "Yeah, me, too. If I'm late for English, Mr. Tordy will be too happy to give me detention."

"Ugh, Mr. Tordy is the worst," Sasha adds.

"So I'll see you in the cafeteria?" Franklin asks me.

I really don't want Sasha hearing this conversation, but since she's looking from me to him, her perfectly arched dark eyebrows lifting in curiosity, I don't have much of a choice. Why can't she just go away? She makes me too uncomfortable. Actually, both of them being so close and talking to me as if we've known each other forever is uncomfortable.

"Sure," I say in the hopes that he'll go on to class and take Sasha with him.

"Cool. See ya, Sasha," he says as he turns and walks away.

"Bye, Franklin."

I turn to go into my class but know that isn't going to work. Sasha's hand on my shoulder stops me.

"I need you to come with me," she says.

"What? No. It's time for class."

"This is more important than class."

"You're crazy. I'm not cutting with you."

"Krystal, you don't understand. This is important."

I'm shaking my head, still refusing to get caught up in what she's saying. By now the hallway is practically empty because the second bell is about to ring. That's the one that tells you you're late and you'd better get your butt in gear before you're caught out of class.

"Get off me, I'm going," I say and pull away from her.

But something keeps me from moving; something keeps me from turning away. I'm not sure what it is, but it's there.

"Fine," Sasha says, then takes a couple steps back from me. I see her look around real quick and I do the same. When I return my attention to her, she's gone.

She didn't disappear.

I know she didn't because that's impossible.

Human beings that are about five feet three inches tall and maybe a hundred or so pounds do not simply disappear into thin air.

Maybe she ran away. Really fast. Faster than the speed of light? That isn't possible either. Sasha is *not* Supergirl.

Today's biology lesson picks up where we left off on Friday with diffusion, osmosis and cell membranes. I have no idea what Mr. Lyle is saying, since my mind is totally not on work.

One minute Sasha was there, asking me to come with her, and the next she was gone. Vanished.

No. Not possible.

Okay, just calm down and be rational. Try to keep this in perspective. She was there and then she was gone. She was going to be late for class, both of us were. So it's logical that she did simply run away. What's not logical is the fact that I saw no trace of her in the long hallway that stretched toward the next turn that would take her to other classes. Now, I don't know what her first-period class is, let alone where it is in the building. But unless it is the very next class to mine, there's no way she could have run down that hall so fast that I didn't even see her back as she retreated.

My stomach churns, not like hunger churning and not like the nervous jittering I feel when Ricky is around. But like a sort of dread, like I know something is about to happen. Something important.

Are you going to sit here all morning trying to figure out what happened or are you going to finally get a backbone and go see for yourself?

I nearly jump out of my chair at the sound of his voice. My textbook and pen fall to the floor, causing everyone to turn and look at me.

Isabella Jackson is absent today so the chair beside me was empty when I'd come into class. Now, it isn't.

Ricky is sitting there, his elbow propped on the desk, his head resting on his hand as he stares at me. He has bushy eyebrows and right now they are lifted in conjunction with the question he'd just asked.

I open my mouth, about to answer him, when it dawns on me that nobody else sees him sitting there or hears him speaking to me. Clamping my mouth shut, I lean over and scoop up my book and pen.

Mr. Lyle had stopped talking at the noise I'd caused. Now he simply turns, lifts his arm and begins writing something on the blackboard again.

She's downstairs waiting for you. Her and that boy from the tracks.

I take my pen in hand and position myself to begin taking notes. We'd have a quiz at the end of the week and I'd no doubt fail since I'm not paying attention.

I think they have something to tell you. Something that might help you.

I want to scream at him to shut up. To leave me alone and let me get on with my normal, disaster-filled life. But I know that I can't. Even if I could, he probably wouldn't listen. In the few conversations I've had with Ricky Watson I've quickly come to realize that he doesn't take "no" for an answer. Or maybe girls don't tell him "no" that often and that's why he isn't used to it. Either way, he doesn't seem to take my sarcasm to heart and get lost like I tell him to. He sticks it out, determined to get his point across.

In the meantime, he seems to take pleasure in telling me off or being as blunt as he possibly can about my actions, my wardrobe, my life.

All you have to do is get a hall pass and go. It's not going to hurt anything to listen to them. Then you can make up your mind, come back and live in your little shell.

That last comment has me glaring at him. Of course he laughs because he has a warped sense of humor. No matter how cute he is. And in that instant I wonder why someone would kill him.

I turn away from him because the questions are filling up my mind. Who killed Ricky? Why am I the one who has to help him? Where did Sasha go? How does Ricky know they have something to tell me?

And then without another thought, my hand is going up until it's raised high in the air and Mr. Lyle is looking at me impatiently. His dark brown face is grim as he folds long arms across his chest. I gulp, trying to find the nerve to speak. He looks like he's just waiting for me to ask him something so he can shoot it down.

"Yes, Miss Bentley. You have something to contribute to the lesson?"

"Ah." I hesitate and swallow. The entire class is looking at me now. I feel like I have something hanging from my nose or my bra is showing, they're staring with such weird expressions. Then I steal a glance at Ricky and he's waving his hand as if to tell me to get on with it.

"Um, can I be…excused?" I finally manage and clear my throat afterward.

Mr. Lyle's mustache kind of twitches as he presses his thick lips tightly together then moves to his desk and scribbles on a notepad. I get up from my seat and am about to take the slip of paper from him when he attempts to come around the desk and bumps his leg. There's a clinking sound, then muffled laughter from the students. Mr. Lyle is really pissed at me now even though I'm not the one who bumped into the desk. With one hand he's holding the hall pass and with the other he's rubbing the side of his leg near his pocket that looks like it's stuffed full of something, keys probably. I hurriedly take the hall pass from his hands before he can say another word or I change my mind.

The minute I'm outside the classroom, the door shut behind me, I'm too afraid to move. For one, I don't know where I'm going. And for two, Sasha and Jake don't know me. What could they possibly have to tell me? Unless it's something about Ricky, about his killer. But how would they know to tell me? I wonder if they're ghost whisperers, too.

I know he's there even though I don't see him. Since there's nobody else in the hallway I just ask, "Do you know what they want with me? Is it about you?"

He's right beside me now. *I don't know. I just know that they're waiting for you and they seem pretty hyped about talking to you.*

"If you know that much, how come you couldn't just hang around and hear what they're saying? That way you could just tell me what they want."

Because I'm not on your payroll.

I stop walking at his smart retort. "And I'm not on yours. So if this has something to do with what you want from me then it'll have to wait until I've decided whether or not to help you."

You haven't decided yet? What, am I, like, on probation?

"No. According to your story, you're stuck between here

and eternity. And you need me to get you there, so if I were you I'd be a little more polite."

Polite? Man, please, that's why you're walking around in a funky mood all the time. Somebody should have snapped you out of this Lifetime network depression a long time ago.

"I am not depressed!" I shout as I stop walking and turn to face him.

Yeah, you are. And for a spoiled brat that's like the end of the world.

I take a step toward him and he starts to smile.

What? Are you going to hit me because I pissed you off?

Ooh, it is so tempting. But could I punch a spirit? With my luck, probably not. "Forget it," I say with more exasperation than I want him to hear. "I don't even know where I'm going."

They're in the basement, by the boiler room.

I almost ask how he knows but keep my mouth shut. Ricky is getting on my nerves. I think about this as I stomp through the exit doors and down the stairs. He is right behind me but I am through talking to him. I am also through listening to him.

Because more and more what he says sounds too much like right.

nine

"**You're** sure she saw you?"

"Duh. Yes, I'm sure. She was standing right next to me. How could she not have seen me?"

Jake makes a sound that seems like he isn't really feeling Sasha's dramatics. He actually sounds worried, which I should be since I'm the one ducking under and around pipes spewing steam all over the place. What kind of people meet in a boiler room?

Anyway, I keep walking toward the voices, wanting to get to them and get this over with as soon as possible. They're still a couple of steps away and they both have their backs turned to me. When I trip on something and start my descent to the floor, the last thing I expect is for Jake to appear instantly, wrapping his arm around my waist and lifting me up before I actually kiss the floor.

"Hey, be careful down here," he says, his voice cracking like he's going through puberty.

I am about to ask him how he got to me so quickly when Sasha walks up to us.

"You came. Great," she says with a smile I swear is permanently etched into her face. Kind of like the Joker on Batman, but not as weird-looking and definitely not with that grotesque makeup. Actually, Sasha's makeup looks good, perfect. Words I immediately associate with her entire persona.

"I need to get back to class." I hear myself and cringe at how weak that sounds. I'm in the tenth grade, with a hall pass. I've got permission to be out of class. Not to be in the boiler room with two other kids, but that's just being picky.

"We really need to talk," Jake says.

That's when I notice he still has his arm around my waist. I make a move to get out of his grasp but my feet feel weird. I look down at them and gasp. They're not touching the floor.

"Oh. Ah, sorry," Jake says then lowers me to the floor.

Okay, now this is just too strange. First Sasha disappears, then Jake, who by the way is only about five inches taller than me and probably fifteen pounds heavier, lifts me into midair and just holds me there. Talk about *Freaky Friday,* except today's Monday.

I start looking around, past Sasha and past Jake, to the one person down here who I think is normal—normally dead. I don't see him. Ricky picks the oddest times to appear and disappear. I wonder if he's hovering above somewhere, hidden in the pipes maybe, just watching and listening.

To my right Jake makes a move. He lifts his hoodie over his head and tosses it to the floor. Beneath it he wears only a white T-shirt. Rolling up the sleeve, he turns to the side and taps his right arm. I look because I'm assuming that's what he wants me to do and, damn, he has the exact same birthmark as me.

"And," Sasha says, lifting her shirt so that her stomach is showing.

So I could see the same *M*-shaped birthmark on her right side. The same one I've had all my life. The one Jake has on his arm.

I look back up to both of their faces. They're staring at me as if I should say something. I can't. I'm too stupefied to speak. What is it with this mark? Why do we all have it? And why do I even care? I should go back to class. Leave the ghost, the spitting steam pipes and these two weirdos behind.

"Yeah, I know, totally strange, right?" Jake says. "But it means something. I'm sure of it."

"He's right," Sasha says, turning back to me. "It means we're all connected. That we all can do things."

I know I must look like a total idiot, standing there with steam shooting out behind me, my mouth hanging open but no sound coming out.

"I...I...can't do anything," I finally manage to say.

"I think you can," Sasha says.

Then I ask, although I already know the answer and because lately I seem to be a glutton for punishment, "What can you do?"

She smiles, her white teeth a smooth contrast against her olive skin. "This."

Then, to my horror, just like she did in the hallway, Sasha disappears. I spin around looking for her and when I get back to my original spot, she's there again.

"You," I start to speak, shaking my head in disbelief even though I know what I just saw. "You can disappear?"

She nods her head, smiling like I'd just complimented her. "I can disappear from one place and reappear in another."

"It's called teleportation," Jake offers.

"Jake's got it, too."

I turn around so fast I almost fall, but Sasha's hand on my elbow keeps me steady. Jake looks around, for what I have no clue. He reaches out suddenly and grabs one of the pipes from the ceiling. I gasp, expecting any moment to either have more steam spewing throughout the humid space or water to spray all of us. Neither happens and Jake proceeds to bend said pipe until it's in the shape of, what else, an *M*.

"Jake's superfast and superstrong," Sasha informs me.

Too strange. I can't handle it. I jump at the sound of Jake dropping the pipe to the floor and move away from both of them. "What are you?"

Jake slips his hands into his pocket. "I think the better question is, what are we?"

"I've got to go," I say, turning away from them, from whatever this is.

"You can't go," Sasha says, pulling on my arm again.

God, I'm sick of people pulling on me these days. I yank away with more force than I mean to, but it's okay because I want her to know I'm serious. "I can and I am. This is… It's…" I can't seem to find the word.

"It's weird. We know," Jake says, lifting one of his hands from his pocket to scratch his head. His hair's too long for a boy, touching the collar of his shirt and curling over.

"But the thing is, we've known for a few months now. Ever since we turned fifteen, to be exact. My birthday is in July," Sasha adds.

"Mine's is August first."

They both look at me like I'm supposed to chime right in. But my mind's moving awfully fast so I already know where this is going. "I turned fifteen July 31st." If they were saying what I thought they were saying, which was that these freaky powers came when they hit high school, then I was definitely not connected to them. The first time I heard a ghost I was in elementary school.

"Hmm, a summer baby thing." Sasha's biting her bottom lip.

"No, it's more like a creepy thing, for psycho people. I'm leaving."

I've taken about five steps when Jake's voice stops me.

"So, you're saying there's nothing weird happening to

you? There's nothing you can do that nobody else can, that nobody else should be able to do. You can tell us, Krystal."

I shake my head. I couldn't tell them, just like I couldn't tell Janet or anybody else.

"We're not here to judge you. We're just trying to figure out what's going on."

Sasha sounds so calm, so matter-of-fact, like all this was as normal as summer vacations and hideous prom dresses.

Then I'm whispering; it's familiar as it rolls through my mind and out of my mouth before I can think to stop it. "I can't hear them, I can't see them, they're not real." My mantra rings in my mind.

"Who's not real?"

I spin around at the sound of Sasha's voice directly behind me. Did I say that out loud? I know I was thinking it. I've been thinking it for days, since Ricky first followed me home from the bus stop. But considering he'd visited me every day since then, and that I'd actually met his girl-friend—both of whom are dead—my little chant method couldn't possibly be working.

"Nothing," I say quickly.

"You said you can't see them. Who don't you see?" Jake had moved closer so that they were now both standing on either side of me, blocking me in.

My chest tightens and I lift my hand to rest over my heart trying to still its abnormal thumping. My throat feels dry like it's stuffed with cotton. I can't possibly talk, can't possibly answer their questions.

But what if they're right?

What if I'm not the only one who's not normal?

They're both eyeing me, Sasha folding her arms over her chest and Jake just staring at me with those eyes that look like a lost puppy. I'm trapped. They know. I might as well come clean. Right?

So I take a deep breath and figure if they even think to tell a soul about what I'm about to say, I'll retaliate by telling that they're hiding in boiler rooms, disappearing and moving things with their eyes. Yeah, and we'll all be wheeled away to the nearest nuthouse.

"Ghosts," I blurt out, afraid that if I stall another minute I won't be able to say it. "Well, the online definition calls them spirits."

"What?" Sasha asks.

Jake takes a step closer to me, his hand going to my elbow. "You see ghosts? You're clairvoyant?"

"Ah." I swallow again and fold my arms over my chest like Sasha had hers. Jake keeps touching me. It's eerie and it's making me more nervous than I already am. "Um, yeah. I'm all those 'clair' things. I can see, hear, sense and converse with spirits of the dead."

Sasha tilts her head and smirks, like she doesn't believe me. "That's not a superpower."

"Where do you see them? At graveyards and stuff?"

I shake my head, not liking Sasha's attitude but touched by Jake's quick trust in my words.

"No. Anywhere."

"Wow. Awesome! A real live medium. Do they ask you for help? Can they hear you? Are any down here right now?"

"She's lying," Sasha claims. This is the first time I've seen her not smile, like her whole mood has changed instantly.

Okay, so now here comes the drama. This is why I stay to myself, why friendship and connections are such a no-no in my book. Girls are catty by nature, Janet told me that when I first started elementary school. Even if I didn't try, there'd always be some type of competition between girls. So now, even though I didn't tell her to invite me down to this sweaty boiler room and even though I don't know how she ever saw the birthmark on my neck or why she thought it was okay to approach me, Sasha and I were at odds.

She had what she called a superpower; she was convinced that I did, too. But when I tell her what I can do, she calls me a liar.

Not happening.

"Look, I didn't come to you, you came to me. So if you don't believe what I'm saying, that's just too damn bad." I take an aggressive step toward her, pointing my finger at her as if there were somebody else in the room and I wanted to make sure she knew I was talking to her. Actions that seem out of character for me but feel really good.

Sasha doesn't move a muscle. She does arch an eyebrow, the right side of her mouth curving up into a half smile, half smirk. "Prove it."

"What? How am I going to prove to you that I see and hear spirits when you don't see or hear them? That's just ridiculous."

"She's got a point, Sasha," Jake says, then clears his throat after Sasha gives him the evil eye.

"Name a ghost you've seen and tell us what they said to you."

"How does that prove anything, if I name somebody you don't know?"

"She's..."

"Shut up, Jake. I don't need you to tell me she's got a point. But we've proved our power to you, you've got to do something to prove yours."

"I don't have to do anything."

Tell them I'm here.

Oh, great, now he decides to appear.

I sigh heavily, seeing Ricky walk right through one of those big fat pipes. The steam halos around him so he looks like he's in one of those gruesome zombie movies, only his face looks a lot better.

"One's here right now," I say because I'm sick of Sasha looking at me with doubt.

Jake immediately looks around the room. "Where?"

"Over there." I point to the pipes. "He's wearing jeans and a T-shirt, boots and an earring."

"He sounds like a thug," Sasha quips. She doesn't want to believe me but I see her eyes darting around the room trying to check things out.

Tell them my name.

I shrug. "His name's Ricky Watson."

Sasha's mouth opens then snaps shut.

"The hip-hopper?" Jake asks in a whisper.

"That's what he says."

Ask them if they know anything about what happened to me.

This has got to be the craziest week I've ever had. No, correct that, the craziest year. Rolling my eyes isn't going to change things. That'll only make me look more lame in Sasha's eyes. Not that I care what she thinks of me. She's the one with the disappearing thing going on.

"Ricky says he needs my help to find out what happened to him. That he can't, like, cross over to the other side if I don't prove he wasn't killed by his friends or something like that. So, do you guys know anything about that?"

Sasha and Jake both exchange bizarre looks.

"Yeah, that's what I thought. Like I said before, I'm outta here."

"Wait!" Sasha screams. "If he's contacting you then we've got to help him. It's like our job or something, right, Jake?"

Jake's head is already bobbing up and down, thick locks of brown hair falling into his eyes. Man, he needed to go to the barbershop.

"We should start by talking to people he knew. Doesn't he have a brother that goes here?"

"And then we should probably talk to those other guys at the table."

That's what I'm talkin' 'bout. Ricky rubs his hands together, his tongue snaking out to run across his bottom lip. *You should have hooked up with these two sooner, they're about business.*

"What?" I say and am both flattered and creeped out when three sets of eyes turn in my direction.

"You two," I say, pointing at Jake and Sasha. "Are you crazy? How are we going to investigate the death of a student? We're not cops. We're tenth graders."

Then I turn to Ricky. "And you. I told you I hadn't decided what to do about you yet, so back off."

Ricky holds up his hands and shakes his head. *Whoa, you feeling yourself now, Krystal. It's about time.*

"Shut up!"

Sasha's shaking her head. "Who? Us?"

"Or the ghost?"

"Arggghhhh!" This is too much. Too insane. This time instead of announcing it, I just turn and walk toward the door.

"Hey, wait up. You can't just leave," Sasha says. "Unless you're afraid to accept your destiny."

My hand's on the doorknob. I turn it and pull the door open a bit. "Don't try to psych me out. I'm not afraid of you or of dead boy over there. But I don't have time to pretend like we're private investigators. I've gotta get back to Biology."

"Actually, I agree with Sasha. There's got to be a reason we have these powers." Both he and Sasha are way too pumped about this power thing.

I wave away his comment like that'll make it mean less. "Whatever."

"You can't run from it, you know. It's not going to go away."

See, I'm not the only one trying to tell you that running's not the answer.

These two never quit. I put my hands over both ears and close my eyes. Counting to ten, I open them again and say in a voice as calmly as I can muster, "I am not running and I am not doing this right now. So I'd like for all of you, living and dead, to leave me alone!"

As I turn and walk away I hear Sasha's last comment. "She needs to take a chill pill."

No, what I need is another life, one where I'm not going insane and kids with marks and spirits with attitude aren't giving me grief.

ten

SO my day has been officially shot. I'd say to hell, but I'm not sure this sort of thing goes on down there.

Supernatural powers.

Supposed to help a ghost.

What kind of foolishness is this? And why do I seem to be dropped right in the middle of it?

Concentrating in any of my classes is out of the question; all my notes consist of idle lines and questions that don't relate to any of the subjects. Questions that I know nobody has the answers to. At lunchtime I go to the library. Yeah, Ricky would say running again. This time I call it hiding. I don't want to see Sasha and Jake, don't want to be near those weirdos. So I sit way in the back, pull the hood of my jacket up over my head and lie down on the desk. I try to put it all out of my mind. But that is pointless because when I close my eyes, I see them—Sasha and Jake—with their marks that look just like mine. I see us, all three of us standing together, looking as if we have a purpose, a reason for being born.

Then I see darkness. I see Ricky and all those dead bodies from my dream the other night, complete with the black smoke that threatened to choke me and the woman on the beach in the white dress who I can still hear crying. My breathing speeds up.

I can talk to spirits. I can see them and hear them. Can I help them?

Do I even want to?

Just so you know, he wasn't the kind of kid everybody said he was. Ricky, I mean.

I jump up so fast I almost fall off the chair. Looking around quickly to make sure nobody had seen me, I try to right myself and adjust the hood on my head. I stuck my earbuds in hoping that all the outside noise would be drowned out. I didn't want to hear the school bells, the kids moving about, the normalcy around my chaotic state.

Yet I heard her loud and clear. I look to my left and there she is, sitting her translucent butt on the edge of the desk beside me, her legs crossed, arms folded over her chest.

It is Trina, Ricky's girlfriend.

"Go away," I whisper, checking around the room to make sure nobody is close enough to hear or see me, talking to myself.

Nope. Since I know you can hear and see me I'm not going away.

"I don't have time for this crap," I say, turning my head away from her.

Don't be such a whiner. Ricky needs your help. And even though I couldn't care less about your spoiled, stuck-up ass, I'm here to ask you to do what you can for him.

"You're his girlfriend, why don't you help him?" I snap, then feel really stupid being jealous of a spirit.

She's a cute ghost, though, with her curly black hair and copper highlights. I asked Janet about getting my hair dyed last year. Of course she told me I was being too grown and brushed me off. Hence, my hair is still the same dark brown as it was when I was born.

She kind of chuckles. *Believe me, if I could I would.*

Ricky was always there for me. Always helping me out of a jam. I should have listened to him, should have taken his warnings seriously.

"I'm sure you gave him enough when you could."

She's on the other side of me now, so I can see her. She's leaning against a bookshelf, her hands behind her back. Her jeans are, like, skintight with a huge silver-buckled belt—that must be for decoration only because those pants are definitely not falling down—around her waist. Her shirt is tight, too, hugging her chest so that it puffs up in honey-toned mounds over the collar of her shirt. She looks hot. That's probably why she was Ricky's girlfriend.

She's also glowing.

There's this bright haze around her body like she's there but not really, almost a shimmer instead of a solid-looking figure. That's how the lady on the beach looked. Ricky doesn't look like that when he appears. I wonder why.

Ricky underestimates you. He said you were young and naive. But I don't think so. I think you're more mature than he realizes.

"I think you should mind your dead-ass business!" I snap because she's getting on my nerves. Ricky doesn't know me and neither does she.

This time she laughs loud. So loud I look around like I think somebody else might hear. Oops, I forgot I'm the resident medium, meaning I'm the only lunatic that can hear her. Just so happens, I'm the one she's laughing at. Ain't that a trip.

Yeah, you've got a little spunk in you. Too bad you're so into yourself you can't use that to help somebody else.

"Why should I help him? I don't even know him. I don't even know how to help."

Then I think about what I am saying, like I am seriously considering helping Ricky get to the other side, or wherever he is supposed to be. Flashes of *Poltergeist* enter my mind.

That tiny woman with those huge sunglasses on standing in front of the door with all that light, telling Carol Anne's mother to go in and get her daughter. I wonder if I'd have to do something bizarre like that. God, I hope not.

"Wait a minute," I say, having another quick thought. "Why are you here? Are you stuck on this side, too?" Maybe her and Ricky are trying to get a two-for-one deal. If that is the case, I definitely don't do hookups!

Nah, I died before Ricky and went on without a glitch.

"So why didn't he?"

She shrugs, which only makes her hair bounce off her shoulders, her gold earrings sparkle and her face look prettier than I want to admit.

I don't know. At first I thought he was just being stubborn, but even when I try to get him to walk with me, he can't.

"What? Walk with you where?"

It's kind of complicated.

"And talking to spirits isn't? If you want my help then I want information." I think. I mean, how much do I really want to know about the afterlife?

All right, well, it's like this. You die and then there's like this break in the road you're taking. You go one way and it leads you to what I figure now is eternity. Like where you're supposed to spend the rest of your afterlife. You go the other way and it's a dead end. You don't go anywhere, you just stay dead.

"That makes absolutely no sense at all," I say, then realize that seeing and talking to a ghost isn't high up there on the intelligence list either.

It does, I'm probably just not explaining it right. Anyway, Ricky's stuck. He said you can help him and I believe him.

I sigh. "I don't know how to prove who killed him."

You can start by talking to Twan and the other guys. I think they know something.

"I can't do this."

Can't or won't?

She doesn't wait for my answer but huffs and disappears. Is there such a thing as a temperamental spirit?

I am so late.

Because of my screwed-up day I totally forgot about meeting with Mrs. Lightner, the guidance counselor. Technically I should have gotten a pass from last period like Mrs. Lightner suggested. Instead I'd spent last period ignoring Alyssa's and Camy's gibes and not paying a bit of attention to Mrs. Tremble's lesson, for the second class in a row.

So as soon as the final bell rings and I am on my way to my locker to grab my stuff and head for the bus stop, I remember the stupid appointment and run like hell to get to the first-floor administrative offices. Unfortunately, Mrs. Lightner had already gone.

So now I'm on my way back down the hall, heading to the front door so I can hopefully catch the bus home. Although I'm not playing any sport or involved in any other after-school activity they should still let me on the bus. God, I hope so.

The halls are empty, which seems strange. I'm so used to them being crowded with kids all the time. Yet the quiet is kind of calming after the past couple of days I've had. The main hallway, once you leave the administrative corridor, splits into two directions. If I turn to the left I'm headed toward the cafeteria and the library. To the right and it's the gymnasium on one side and the auditorium on the other. I keep walking straight, toward the twin sets of double doors that will, thankfully, take me right outside to the bus stop.

Then I feel it.

Like this chill moving through my body. It starts at my ankles and quickly winds its way upward until I stop moving and shiver. Weird.

I pull my jacket closer around my chest, adjust my book bag and purse then make like I'm heading for the door again.

And I hear it.

Crying. Somebody's crying.

I know I should keep on going out the door, my mind is screaming that I do so. Remember the last time I followed the sound of crying, ghost beach lady scared the bejesus out of me. Of course my feet are, like, detached from brain communication and instantly have me turning, heading in the direction I hear the crying.

Noises are coming from the gym. Sneakers squeaking across the floor, a steady pounding, then a couple of yells and a whistle blowing. Basketball practice.

But even over that hoopla, the crying echoes in my head. I keep walking right past the gym through the swinging doors that lead to the locker rooms. That hallway's empty but the crying is getting louder. So I keep walking.

To say that I've completely flipped would probably be an understatement. Here I am wandering through the halls after school hours looking for someone who's crying. Someone who's crying pretty doggone loud since I heard it from all the way near the front door and now I'm close to the equipment room.

It stinks down here. Smells like sweat and funk. I wave a hand in front of my face as I continue on inside. Not only can I hear the crying loudest from here, but that chilliness in my body is starting to warm up a bit.

Still I don't see anybody and I'm about to give up this stupid chase and head home like I should be. But as I turn around to head back toward the door I see her.

All the way in the corner, stuffed between the two floor-to-ceiling shelves holding basketballs, soccer balls and whatever other sports paraphernalia that could be squeezed into the small compartments. She's sitting on the floor, her arms wrapped around legs pulled up to her chin. Her head's down but I know it's a she because of the long red hair hanging around her like a blanket.

I take a step toward her. Her head shakes as she continues to cry, loud, wrenching sobs that make me extremely uncomfortable. As I get closer, of course I'm wondering why she's in here, what could have happened to her and what in the world I can possibly do for her. I'm focused on the body, the sounds echoing from it, my legs taking me closer and closer without my mind's permission.

Then, as if she hears my approach, her head shoots up and eyes big as saucers and dark as night look up at me. She opens her mouth, baring chipped and bloody teeth, and yells, *Go away!*

Okay, now my mind has some control and I stumble backward bumping into some boxes I hadn't even known were behind me. My bag and purse fall to the floor as I stumble to keep myself upright. My heart's in my throat, the intense thumping almost clogging it so I can't speak right away.

Go away, I said! the girl repeats.

"Ah." I hear myself stuttering, my feet plant themselves in the spot where I stand, rejecting the run-like-hell thoughts in my head. "What happened to you? Um, is there someone I can call to come and get you?"

The minute I say that, I know how stupid it sounds. Her hair's matted against her head and her eyes, they don't look quite right. And let's not forget the blood trailing down her chin, mixing with the tears that streak her chalky face.

Nooooooo! she sort of yells and moans.

In front of me, my hands are clenched, fingers wringing around each other. What the hell am I doing here? What am I supposed to do?

"Did somebody hurt you?" I ask impulsively.

Her head tilts to the side, like she's thinking about what I just said. *You know who hurt me! You know! Everybody knows but nobody cares! Nobody cares!*

With the last words she, the one I now know for sure is a spirit, stands up and leans her scary-ass face into mine. *Nobody cares!*

Now I do what I guess I should have done like two seconds ago. I scream like somebody's beating me. Only the spirit must think that's cute because she screams, too. Now we're both screaming, her in my face and me wondering what I ever did to my feet to make them disobey like this.

"Krystal! Krysal! What's the matter?"

I feel the hands on my arms, pulling at me, trying to turn me around. Then I look into familiar eyes that have me closing my mouth, ending at least my screams. The horrendous sounds of spirit girl are still shrilling through the air.

"Do you hear her? Do you see her? She's crying and she's—" She's a ghost, you idiot, why are you asking if Jake can see or hear her? My lips clamp shut as he continues to stare at me.

After a few seconds I move out of his grasp. "I'm okay," I whisper and wish it were true.

I'm leaning over, trying to catch my breath, my hands resting on my knees, when Sasha kneels down in front of me.

"Who was she?"

I shake my head. "I don't know. She didn't look…familiar," I say, searching for the right words.

"Did she ask you to help her?" Jake asks from behind me.

"No." I stand upright and inhale deeply, closing my eyes

for a second then reopening them. "No, she didn't seem to want my help. She seemed…angry."

"At you?"

I shrug then move to where I'd dropped my bags. It hits me then that her screaming has stopped. I look to the spot where she'd last been and she is gone. I walk over and look between the shelves. She isn't there either.

"I don't think it was at me personally. I asked her if someone had hurt her and she said that I knew. That everyone knew and nobody cared," I say, remembering her exact words coupled with the stark fear that rippled from her body to mine. In that moment, I'd felt it, the second she'd gotten close up on me I felt her fear. And it was terrifying.

"Come on, let's get you out of here," Jake says, wrapping an arm around my shoulders. Normally I don't like people touching me but this is Jake. And a few feet away is Sasha. We three have something in common, something we have no idea about, but still it is a link.

Grabbing my bags, we all start walking to the door.

"We need a game plan," Jake says the minute we are in the hallway.

"What?" I say. I'm the one who just saw the freaky-ass spirit and he's talking about a plan.

"This might be connected," he says.

"Connected to what?"

Maybe it is the pitch of my voice or I probably look at him like he is crazy, but anyway, Jake drops his arm from my shoulders and takes a step away from me. He always seems to be touching me. But as soon as I notice he stops, like he's been caught doing something wrong. "Two ghosts have come to you for help in the past two days. I don't think that's a coincidence," he says.

Sasha flicks her long curly hair over one shoulder and

adds, "I agree. They both need your help, probably with the same problem."

That's just great, another one of Ricky's chicks I have to deal with. I really didn't want to agree with them, but what they're saying makes sense.

Yeah, I think you need a plan, Ricky chimes in. He's leaning against the wall near the gym, his hands stuffed in the pockets of his jeans.

My reaction to seeing him at this very moment is swift. "Well, I think you need to figure out who's helping you, me or Trina or...or...whoever crying girl was in there," I snap and immediately feel the heat of embarrassment in my cheeks.

Jake and Sasha are looking at me.

"I think she's talking to the dead guy," Sasha says in a singsongy voice, barely moving her mouth, looking and sounding as ridiculous as I probably do.

"Where is he?"

Jake's immediately looking up and down the hallway. He really wants to see a spirit. He has no idea that if I could I'd give him this creepy power in a heartbeat. I huff, "He's over there." I point to where Ricky is standing across from us.

Don't worry about Trina, she's just trying to help out. She can't get me through so she wants you to do it.

"Why? So you two can live happily ever after? I'm not into fairy tales, you know. And just who is this other chick?"

Damn, girl, what is your problem? If you're not complaining about one thing, you're arguing over another. I don't even know that girl in there, he says, pointing toward the equipment room.

I fold my arms over my chest and realize two things: (1) I'm jealous of two female ghosts because Ricky may or may not know them, and (2) Sasha and Jake are witnessing a one-sided conversation. Am I living in Lincoln, Connecticut, or Freakyville?

Only one way to deal with this without further embarrassing myself in front of these people. "Okay, look, I've gotta get home or Janet will send out a search party." I start walking toward the doors again.

"Sasha will take you home," Jake offers.

Sasha mumbles something but I can't see her nor do I care what she said. "That's okay, I'll get the bus."

"Bus has already left," Jake says.

"My car's around the other side," Sasha says as we approach the doors. "That's where I'm heading, all those riding with me better follow along."

I look at Jake who's got this pleading kind of look in his eyes, then mumble, "Great. Just great."

He is the polar opposite of Sasha. I mean, besides being a boy and all. But Jake's not pushy and he's not bossy. He kind of just goes with the flow. Sasha, however, is moody and grates on my nerves. She's pushy and controlling but is soon going to find that I'm not a Lincoln-bred girl. I'm straight from the city and will knock her out if need be.

Take the ride with Sasha and stop being so stubborn.

I cut my eyes at Ricky as we hit the doors. I'm already walking behind Jake, following along just like Ms. Sasha said. So I'm ignoring Ricky because my head is hurting and my stomach is doing funny things. A cross between the heated ball I feel when I'm around Janet and those stupid butterflies fluttering whenever I see him. And let's not forget the fear from crying girl, that's still churning around inside of me like a cruel reminder that I'm not normal.

I don't want this power.

I don't want to help spirits.

I don't want to be friends with other kids with powers.

Hell, I don't know what I want anymore.

eleven

well, I calm down enough to let Sasha drive me home. She has a cute little car, a red BMW. I should have expected nothing less than a sporty vehicle for her majesty. What I don't expect is the huge guy that she calls Mouse who is supposed to be her driver.

Mouse looks like Shaquille O'Neal on steroids—yeah, he's that big. I know he has to be more than seven feet tall. How he squeezes himself into Sasha's teeny-tiny car I don't know, but he does, right beside me. His head is bald, his skin the darkest I've ever seen. His eyes seem quiet, not mean or anything.

I sit in the back because being in her car is enough; I don't really think I could stand sitting right up front with her during the drive home.

"Wow, great house," Jake says as we pull up in front of my house.

I glance out the window while waiting for the car to come to a complete stop. Looking at it in the low sunlight of late afternoon, I guess it is kind of cool. It's a mixture of stones and shingles in the front, in shades of brown. The wraparound porch is what I really think makes it cool. The front yard, which had a lot of dirt mounds in it just the other day, now has neat rows with small budding flowers. Janet has been out today.

I don't know if that is a good or bad thing so I dismiss it. Tapping on the back of the seat Jake is sitting in, I say, "Can you let me out?"

He reaches for the door handle when Sasha stops him with a look. Then her frosty dark gaze comes back to me.

"We really need to get together to talk about this. How about we meet at my house around eight?"

"I can't tonight," Jake speaks up. "It's just me and Pop Pop on Monday nights. Dad's got bowling."

"Okay, then we'll come to your place," Sasha says. "Deal?"

She's looking at me and I want to say, "No, it's not a deal because we don't need to meet." But all the way home I've been thinking that maybe Ricky picked me for a reason. I mean, there has to be more than one medium in the world. Right? (Okay, so I searched the Net again last night trying to figure out exactly what my superpower is and since I can do all of those "clair" things, it stands to reason that a better term for my power is a medium—one who can see and communicate with spirits.)

Maybe Ricky only picked me because I go to Settlemans High and have easier access to the clique his brother hangs with. Then why did that girl contact me? Why was her crying meant for me to hear? And who was the woman on the beach? Was she connected in some way? I kind of thought not since she didn't speak to me at all.

Whatever the reason, I think I like that somebody needs me. For the past few months I've felt so displaced, so inconsequential, that maybe now I can make a difference. To a spirit. Or to the person this spirit used to be. Maybe?

"I don't know, I'll have to see if I can make it. It's a school night and I'm not usually out at that time." Who am I kidding—since moving to Lincoln, I haven't been out of this house except to go to school and wherever Gerald convinced Janet he wants us to go as a so-called family. Then again, if I tell Janet I'm going to a friend's house she'll probably be so excited she'll offer to drive me herself.

"Tell your parents we're going to watch a movie for class tomorrow. I'll come by and pick you up around quarter to eight and we can head over to Jake's."

I'm getting out of the car as she's talking. When I stand on the curb, I look back at her and shrug. "Okay, I guess."

I rush through my homework because, let's face it, I don't really know what I am doing anyway, having not paid a bit of attention in class today. Still I figure part of an effort is better than no effort at all. That will definitely be reflected in the fifty percent I'll get as a homework grade tomorrow, instead of the zero I would have scored had I not bothered to do anything at all. I'm proud of myself for making the right decision and not overly concerned with the fact that come test time I'll still be out of luck.

Anyway, I go downstairs to have dinner with the adults of the household. I really couldn't bring myself to call them parents, not even Janet.

Of course, Gerald isn't there. So what else is new? Really, I just don't know why Janet married him. I guess it was money. But we weren't doing so bad by ourselves. We did better with Daddy.

Tonight's meal is, to my surprise, pizza! And it is from one of those delivery places because the boxes are still on the table. Janet sits in her usual seat, with one lone slice of pepperoni pizza on her plate, and looks up like she's been waiting for me.

So I pick up my plate and move a little farther down the table to the box and lift it up. My stomach is doing somersaults and growling like it's been empty for days. But when I pick up a slice and put it on my plate I get a good whiff of the pizza and start to feel like I'm gonna hurl. So I ditch the idea of a second slice and just sit down hoping I can eat the first one.

One bite and I'm chewing, letting the taste of cheese mixed with spicy pepperoni and tangy tomato sauce settle in my mouth. It brings back memories and my chewing slows down. And when I go to swallow, the food actually feels like it's stuck. I take several big gulps in an attempt to push it down and when it still doesn't move I pick up my glass of water and take huge gulps of that, too.

Finally the food moves, traveling down my throat and into my stomach with heat that almost makes me cry. I sit there for a minute, just staring at what used to be my favorite food, wondering when I'll be normal again. Probably never.

"I'm picking you up early from school tomorrow," Janet finally says something.

I'm glad she waited until I managed to get that food down or else I would have choked.

"What? Why?"

She's wringing her hands nervously, an action I've seen her do a lot in the past couple of days. "I made an appointment with that doctor I mentioned. The one I think you should talk to."

"For what? There's nothing wrong with me." And the minute I say that I know that there is something wrong. But it's not something I think a head doctor can fix.

"I didn't say there was, baby. Gerald and I just think it would be good if you had someone you could open up to. Share things with."

"I don't give a crap what Gerald thinks!"

Janet gives me a look where one of her eyebrows lifts up higher than the other and her head kind of tilts. I haven't seen it in a while, but it still makes me nervous.

"Like I said, we both think you need to talk to someone.

This depression you're in is getting worse and we want to help you before it's too late."

"Too late?" What in the world is she talking about? "Too late like what? Like you think you're going to open my door one day and find me hanging from the ceiling?" A girl in my sixth-grade class had done that because Johaven Britton kept threatening and punching on her. I used to see her crying in the hallways and I always felt sorry for her, she looked so sad. I don't look like she did so I'm pretty sure that killing myself because I don't like that my mother left my dad and moved us to this small town where I just so happened to meet two people who are weirder than I am is not a possibility.

Janet closes her eyes briefly and when she opens them and looks at me again she looks really sad, like my words really hurt her. "That's not what I said, Krys. I just want you to be okay and I don't know what else to do for you myself. So I figured that maybe somebody else could help you."

"I don't want to go," I say in a voice that sounds sulky and juvenile—I mean elementary-like.

"It's not a choice."

"So what else is new?"

"You know, Krystal, I'm doing the best I can. Sometimes we can't help the hand we're dealt in life and I'm just trying to make the best of what I have. I'm sorry if that's not good enough for you."

My fingers are rubbing along the tablecloth, my chest hurting for some strange reason. "It's just not what I want," I say.

"We don't always get what we want," Janet answers quietly.

"Is that what you told Daddy?" I look up at her and wonder if that sad look she's been giving me will disappear. If she'll turn away from me like she usually does when I talk about Daddy.

This time she doesn't.

But I notice that her eyes are filling with tears.

"No. That's not what I told your father."

"Then why did you leave him?"

She takes a deep breath, those tears that filled her eyes drip down and fall on her cheeks. It looks funny. I don't see my mother cry a lot. My chest hurts more but I still don't understand.

"That's grown folks' business and you are not grown." Gerald's cold voice sounds throughout the room and Janet hurries to wipe her eyes. In the next instant she's jumping up from her chair, going to him and offering her lips for a kiss.

Again, I want to puke.

Gerald's looking at me like he could shake me, or choke me, or at the very least push me out of his way. I always feel like that with him, like I'm bothering him or messing up some plan he had. Not that I care because he's not my father and what he thinks doesn't really matter.

I open my mouth to tell him that this—the conversation between me and Janet—is none of his business but then I see how she's all pushed up on him now and I change my mind. Her fingers are buried in his shirt, her head leaning on his shoulder. She's not looking at me anymore. She got up from the table and left me, just like she left my dad.

So I stand and prepare to leave myself.

"Where are you going? Back to your room?" Gerald says and he sounds all nasty, like one of those villains on TV.

"No," I say, turning back to him with a snap of my head. "I'm going out...with friends."

Janet's head pops up and she looks at me this time. "Friends? What friends?"

And even though she's really not the reason I'm going because she really gets on my nerves, I say her name first, hoping that Gerald will know who I'm talking about.

"Sasha Carrington is coming to pick me up. We're going to another friend's house to watch a movie for a project we're doing in school."

That lie came so easy I didn't even blink.

"Oh. Well, that sounds nice." Janet's wet eyes seem to have dried up instantly. Now she's watching me with an almost smile.

Maybe she's the one that's crazy and not me. I already know that Gerald is not right.

"It's a school night, don't be out too late," he says.

I roll my eyes because that's easier—and probably won't get me punished—than saying what I really want to say.

twelve

Jake's house looks like it's about half the size of ours. It's past the tracks and along the riverbank. The street he lives on is quiet but has a ton of other houses the same size as his all cramped together. It almost looks like a trailer park, except they're real houses.

Sasha's car is so out of place on this street. Still she parks right in front of the house like it's nothing new and we both get out. Mouse climbs out from the backseat. I looked back at him once while riding and saw that his long legs were folded like the chairs in my grandma's basement. Sasha doesn't talk to him or about him, she just acts like he's not there. I feel kind of bad for him. When I turn back, I see him leaning against the car instead of getting in the front to sit. I guess he needs to stretch—I don't blame him.

"Listen, Jake's real sensitive about where he lives and his family and all that. So don't say anything that might hurt his feelings."

I turn away from Mouse because he catches me staring and that makes me feel bad. I'm looking up at Jake's house when I say, "You don't have to tell me that. I'm not a jerk about stuff like this."

"Well, I don't really know you, so I wasn't sure. His dad

works weird hours for the electric company so Jake has to take care of his grandfather a lot."

For her not to know me that well she sure doesn't have a problem telling me Jake's business.

"Where's his mother?" And clearly I don't have a problem asking for more.

Sasha shrugs. "I heard she left. Then my mom said she died. Jake doesn't talk about it so don't even think about asking him."

I figure I'll take her advice, after all she's known him a lot longer than I have.

She keeps walking up the two front steps, her curly hair dancing behind her, then pulls open the creaky old screen door. I admit that she's right, she doesn't know me, and I don't know her or Jake. Yet I'm here, ready to talk about the one thing we all seem to have in common.

Sasha knocks once and before she can pull her arm back Jake opens the door. Light, in a golden haze, pours from the house to the dark outside. He doesn't smile but looks over Sasha's shoulder at me then nods. "Come on in."

I walk behind Sasha, keeping my mouth shut and trying really hard not to look around his house. It feels warm in here. I mean I can instantly feel extra heat. Outside it's about sixty-five degrees. In here feels much hotter. And it smells like old people. Like those mothballs they keep in all the closets and in their drawers. It's not really a stinky smell but it gets in your nose and burns after a while. I remember it from the old folks' home, so it's already bothering me.

Jake's leading the way, walking us past what I think is the dining room. His house is set up like one long hallway and different rooms are on either side. It's kind of hard to keep my head straight ahead and act like I'm not looking around, because I am. That probably means I'm nosy but I'm not real worried about that right now. Unfortunately, my eyes keep wandering so I'm not getting a real good look into every room, just quick glances. Then I see the wheelchair in one room and I completely stop.

I've never seen a wheelchair in person before. Well, except for when I was twelve and went to the nursing home to visit my grandfather. It was creepy in there with all those old people wanting to touch you with their crinkly hands. All the extra voices I was hearing didn't help either. I know now that those voices belonged to dead people. People who had probably died in that nursing home. I wonder if that meant I could only hear the dead in the spot where they died. No, that can't be true, I hear Ricky any and everywhere.

"Come on, Krystal," I hear Sasha say with irritation clear in her voice.

Oh, great, I've been caught standing here staring like some sort of flake.

The room Jake's sitting in has two mattresses on a bed frame in one corner, an old desk and chair in the other and two chairs that look like they might have come from the kitchen right next to the desk. On the desk is a computer, which shocks me because it's the newest-looking thing in this room. I mean, all the furniture and stuff is pretty old, like the kind you see in those shops that only sell old stuff for lots of money. But the computer is the bomb!

It's an iMac with a twenty-four-inch screen. I just know it has everything on it because why else would you buy it if you weren't going to load it up?

"Here, you can sit right here," Jake says.

Sasha has already taken a seat on his bed so he can only be talking to me. I notice he's changed his pants. Earlier he had on jeans but now he's wearing sweatpants. His hair is still a mess, falling all in his eyes so he looks more like an animal than a boy. But I'm not real worried about how he looks. I just want to get this little powwow over with so I can go home.

Home to what? Janet and Gerald, both looking at me like I've just grown another head? No, correction, Janet looking at me like I've grown another head and Gerald looking at me like he could stomp me right into the ground. That can't be normal, for a grown-up to hate a kid that much. But I guess if the kid's not yours you could hate them until hell froze over and nobody would care.

Anyway, I don't want to think about the odd couple right now. I follow Jake's direction and sit in one of the chairs. Again, I'm trying not to look around at the chipping dull beige paint on his walls or the dresser that doesn't have any knobs on it.

I'm really not prejudiced against people who don't have what I have or anything like that. I'm just curious about Jake's life. He seems so quiet and so normal. It's weird that his house isn't all pretty and filled with new stuff, but he seems perfectly happy with who he is and where he's from. While me, on the other hand, can't stand to be in the house Janet works so hard to create and walks around with enough friction in my mind to fill a psych ward. Which, coincidentally, is where Janet and her husband are trying to send me.

"I drew a sketch of our marks," Jake starts, giving me and Sasha a piece of paper. "I figure that's where it all starts, our connection, I mean. Because how many kids have the exact same birthmark on different parts of their body? That's a big coincidence."

I look down at the paper and I must have frowned. I admit, my first thought was that this was one crappy drawing but I would never have said that aloud. Sasha's remark says it is written all over my face.

"Let me guess, you don't like his drawing," she drawls.

My head pops up and I immediately look at Jake. "No. I didn't say that."

"It's okay. I'm not really good at drawing." He reaches

over to the desk and grabs a pad and a pencil. "Here, you do it. Look at mine and draw it."

How does he know I can draw?

Oh, come on. He probably doesn't know but since I'm the one looking at his work like it's below grade level, it stands to reason he's calling me out.

Okay, whatever. I'll just get it over with.

He pulls up the sleeve to his T-shirt and I look at his mark. It's familiar because, like he said, it's identical to mine. And to Sasha's.

So I don't need to keep looking at it but I do. He's got arms like those men on TV, the ones who lift weights and stuff. I mean, he's not buff or anything, but from the way his clothes just hang off him I assumed he was bony. I assumed wrong. My fingers wrap tightly around the pencil as I hold the pad steady with my other hand. Without even looking down I start to draw. My hand is kind of just moving, sliding over the paper as I stare at Jake's arm. It's not all that fancy, this mark that looks like an *M,* but it kind of swirls at the ends. As I'm looking at it now I think it's glowing. Hmm, maybe that's just my overactive imagination—a side effect to being able to see the dead. Maybe now I can see all sorts of strange stuff.

Suddenly Jake hisses like a scared cat. "Jeez, it burns," he hollers. My hand just keeps on moving across the paper. I'm not even really concentrating.

"What burns?" Sasha asks.

I keep drawing even though I'm looking at Jake's face now instead of the mark. His cheeks are turning red, his eyes going wider. He shakes his head and that unruly dark hair flies away so I can see them better. My heart's beating a little faster but I try not to notice. The room feels funny, like somebody turned the heat up even higher and a kernel of sweat starts rolling down my back.

"It's the Power," a voice comes from the doorway.

I don't have to look past Jake to know that it is his grandfather. The sound is so familiar from my one visit to the nursing home. Old people talked with this crackly-like whisper. But it isn't the voice that makes my hand stop drawing and my fingers clench the pencil even tighter.

It was what he'd said.

"What power?" I hear myself ask without a second thought.

"Pop Pop, we're working on a school project. Go back into the living room. *Jeopardy* is about to come on," Jake says, getting up from his chair.

"I don't want to watch *Jeopardy*. I need to tell you about the Power. It's time."

He is wearing a blue shirt with big white flowers—Jake's grandfather, not Jake. It is a button-up shirt and above the top button some of his white hair sticks out. He wears glasses so I can't really see the color of his eyes but his ears are big and he is balding in the center. I figured the wheelchair belonged to him but he is using a cane as he makes his way into Jake's room.

"No, Pop Pop. Not right now," Jake tries to say but his grandfather waves his hand away and keeps right on moving until he finds the chair at the desk and lowers his body in a slow, precise way down onto the seat.

I look over at Sasha to get her take on our visitor and she's looking at me, twirling her finger around as if to say that Jake's grandfather is crazy. I hurry up and look away because I don't want Jake to catch us and think I'm agreeing with her. Still, he looks kind of old so he could have that condition where old people start to forget where they are and who they are.

But I don't know. He's talking about power and we just discovered that all three of us have some kind of power. Like Jake just said a few minutes ago, that's just too coincidental.

"Hi, Mr. Kramer. Do you remember me? I'm Sasha." She's talking ten times louder than she was before and slow like she thinks he doesn't understand English.

Mr. Kramer nods and looks at her. "Sure, I remember you. You're the one with the accent and the fancy car."

I almost smile at that. Sasha did have a slight accent. I couldn't really place it and because we just started talking— like today—I'm not about to ask her any personal questions. Anyway, Jake told me earlier that her mother is from somewhere in Argentina.

"That's right, I'm from South America," she offers.

"No, you're not," Mr. Kramer snaps. "Neither of you are." He looks at me and I figure he thinks I have an accent, too, but I haven't said much for him to know that for sure.

Sasha gives a deep, exasperated sigh and rolls her eyes. "Yes, I am."

"No," Mr. Kramer says adamantly. "Your daddy's from right here in Lincoln. And he was here with your mama."

She pauses like she's thinking about his words. "Yeah, I think she was here for a while. She was born in Buenos Aires, Argentina, and so was I. My dad brought her here, she left when she had me and then she came back later."

Mr. Kramer nods his head, wisps of leftover hair cradle the sides but don't cover the tips of his big red ears. "She was here the year of the storm. All of them were."

Jake just drops his head down as his grandfather talks and Sasha rolls her eyes again.

"Hi…um, Mr. Kramer. I'm Krystal," I say. I want to ask him questions but it's probably polite to introduce myself first. I mean, I am in his house and all that.

His head turns a bit and I think he's looking at me. Those glasses are so thick it's really hard to tell, except that I feel a little jittery like I'm being examined. So I figure he's the one doing the examining. Anyway, he stares at me a few long seconds before he nods his head.

"She was here, too, your mama."

He knows Janet?

I lick my lips, my mouth suddenly dry. My shirt's gonna be wet by the time I leave 'cause, dayum, it's hot in here. "I'm Krystal Bentley and my mother…" Wow, I haven't called Janet that in a while. It sounds funny. "Um, her name's Janet."

He just keeps on nodding. "They were all here."

"Okay, Pop Pop. Both of their mothers were here in Lincoln at one time. Now, you've had your say. Let me take you to your room." Jake jumps up and reaches for his grandfather's arm to help him up.

Mr. Kramer lifts his cane, waves it in front of him so that Jake has a choice—either back up or get swatted in the nuts. Wisely, he chooses to back up. "I'll go to bed when I'm finished. Now you sit down and mind your manners. You're not too big to get your hide tanned."

Sasha giggles. I lift a hand to fan my face. I don't want to see Jake get his hide tanned. I don't even want to see Jake's hide.

Jake looks really embarrassed as he sinks back into his seat. I think he likes that slouched-over position; he always takes it whenever anybody says something to him that shuts him up.

"You know, it snows here in September."

Mr. Kramer starts and I'm beginning to think he really might have that old people's forgetful disease.

The room is eerily quiet and I clench my hands together. Aside from the heat, the house is old and could probably pass for haunted, if you believe in that sort of thing. I mean, everything about it looks decrepit, like it is ready to fall right down around us. That's how haunted houses usually look. This would be a small one, but it could still be haunted.

And why am I even thinking that? Well, because the

golden light that I spotted when Jake had first opened the door is only in the hallway. His room is dimmer, probably because the only lamp in here is supersmall. And like it knows I'm talking about it the light in the lamp flickers. Creepy. Then the windows rattle. Yes, I do mean rattle. It's a chink-chink-chink kind of sound and both me and Sasha turn to look.

"It's windy tonight," Mr. Kramer says. "That's how it starts."

"What? The snowstorms? With all due respect, it's not September, Mr. Kramer," Sasha says.

She is shaken up. I can see it in her hazel eyes, but she would never admit it. Actually she covers it pretty well with her wisecracks.

"No. But when usually doesn't matter. It comes when it wants, stays as long as it feels like and leaves something behind every time."

"What does?" My voice sounds really quiet but in this silence I'm sure everybody hears me.

Again the light flickers and I feel like we should be sitting around the campfire listening to horror stories that will surely keep us all from sleeping tonight. But we're not. We're in Jake's bedroom and his grandfather is acting like he has something to tell us.

I wish he'd get on with it.

"The Power," he says finally.

And I swear the heat I've been feeling since I got here has swirled up my body and wrapped around my neck, all ready to choke the life out of me. At the same time, Jake curses, grabbing his arm. Right where the mark is. I instantly look at Sasha, who is now sitting up on the bed, rocking back and forth.

"It gets stronger when you're together. It feeds from each of you all at the same time. And it will grow."

Suddenly Mr. Kramer's voice doesn't sound like an old

person. It's still kind of crackly but it's not shaky anymore. It's slow, deliberate, clear.

"We each have the Power?" Sasha asks with a smirk.

Mr. Kramer nods. "It came with your birth."

"We're not born on the same day," Jake says.

"But around the same time, I suspect."

I'm already nodding when Sasha answers, "We're born in July, the last week in July. Jake was born the first of August."

"Your mamas, they were all here that night of the storm."

The windows rattle again and I'm seriously thinking of getting the hell out of here. As much as I want to know why I can see and talk to dead people, this is really starting to freak me out.

"The wind started just like that. About two weeks before the storm actually hit. But when it did, it was a doozy."

"Okay, so it snowed when our mothers were here. What does that have to do with us?"

"I didn't say it snowed," he answers sternly. "I said the wind started two weeks before. Then the rain came. It was a lot of rain, a lot of wind. The newsman finally said he thought it was a hurricane."

"Okay, a hurricane in September isn't out of the ordinary," Jake is muttering.

"I didn't say it was in September," Mr. Kramer argues.

I am trying to keep this all straight in my mind, trying to figure out what he is attempting to tell us. I wish he'd just get on with it and stop all this beating around the bush. Somehow, though, I don't think he can help it. "But you said that it snows in Lincoln in September."

Mr. Kramer waves a hand. "That was something else. Has nothing to do with this."

Yeah, he might be more out of touch than I originally thought.

"It was November, the day before Thanksgiving, when the rain and wind started real bad. The newspeople didn't know what was going on. Then the river started rising and some smart guy says he thinks it's a hurricane."

"In November?" I ask, nervous that this conversation is starting to feel like I've had it before. With Franklin, who likes to know things about the weather.

"Yuuup, it was the strangest thing. We had us a full-on hurricane in November. I tell you, houses were blowing around like toys. Cars floating in the river, wind howling so loud you thought it was talking right in your ear."

And his voice goes to a whisper as he says that. If these were theatrics, Mr. Kramer deserved an Oscar for technical work.

"That's when it came."

"When what came?"

"The Power," he says and his eyes get so wide I can actually see them through the thick lenses he wears.

We all get quiet again.

"It came with that storm and that's how you got it."

"But we weren't even born yet," Sasha says.

Jake looks at her, then he looks at me and then the heat I was feeling in my whole body suddenly shifts to my neck. I put my hands back there because it feels like there's fire inside my skin about to burn right through.

Jake hisses again, this time adding a long curse behind it. He's reaching for his arm and my gaze falls to his mark.

I figure it's got to be burning just like mine.

And then it glows.

I don't think I'm imagining it this time. Jake's *M* is now green.

Sasha lets loose the girliest, shriekiest scream I've ever heard as she lifts her shirt.

And you got it, her mark is glowing, too, like a pink neon light just above her hip bone.

I jump up out of my chair, lifting my hair and turning to show them.

"Wow," I hear Jake whisper.

"It's blue," Sasha says.

Mr. Kramer sighs. "The Power. Together. Again."

Jake stands first, stopping in the middle of the floor, his bicep flexing as the *M* glows a fluorescent green. Sasha gets up from the bed, her shirt still pulled up.

"God, it's burning like a bee sting!"

I presume my blue *M* is glowing brighter as I'm now closer to them.

"Great," I speak up first. "We're a trio of weirdos with glowing skin and freaky powers."

"No," Jake says quietly, "Not weirdos. We're misfits."

"That's right!" Mr. Kramer yells and we all turn to him expecting an explanation. Instead he says, "It's time for *Jeopardy*."

Okay, so where that comment came from I have no clue. Neither does Sasha, I can tell by the strange way she looks from Mr. Kramer to me then to Jake, who just shrugs as if this happens all the time.

Mr. Kramer starts to leave Jake's room, but as he does something falls from his pocket. An old, raggedy book that Jake immediately bends down and picks up.

As he turns back to face us I'm not thinking about the book or *Jeopardy* or even the old man in the doorway. I'm thinking about this power and how my life's probably never going to be the same.

Nov. 17, 1932

This has been one crazy couple of months and it all started with the storms. Hurricane season came right on time, just like the weatherman predicted. But nobody said how hard the storms would hit us. Seems like we stayed locked in the house praying more than doing anything else. Except we must have taken a few minutes to do something else.

Today I found out I was expecting a baby. Me and Joseph's first baby. I hope it's a boy.

From the diary of
Eleanor Jean Kramer

thirteen

It is Jake's great-grandmother's diary. It makes perfect sense that he will be the one to keep it, to read it and to share whatever knowledge it might hold about this so-called Power his grandfather talked about.

So it looks like we are now officially on a mission. First, to help Ricky figure out what really happened and then to figure out why the three of us have these powers and what Jake's grandfather meant about them growing.

The clock at the bottom of my computer screen says 2:15 a.m. I should be in bed, fast asleep like the other citizens of boring old Lincoln. Instead I'm sitting in my dark room with only the glow from the computer screen. I inhale deeply and my fingers move across the keyboard again. I've searched all the powers we have, medium, teleportation, superstrength, they all seem pretty valid—as far as super-natural powers go. There are lots more powers but they don't concern me right now. If the powers themselves are proven both by literature and by experience then they have to come from somewhere. Jake's grandfather said it was the weather. Strong storms that hit Lincoln at odd times.

So I type in "strange weather patterns."

Lots of hits, woo hoo!

I search hurricanes first since that was the type of storm that we were supposedly conceived during. Then I key in the year Eleanor Jean Kramer conceived because something tells me that has a lot to do with what is going on now.

The 1932 Atlantic hurricane season ran through the summer and the first half of fall in 1932 in a series of deadly storms.

First: formed on May 5 in the south-central Caribbean Sea. Hit the Gulf of Mexico on May 12.

Second: formed August 11 in the southern Gulf of Mexico near the Yucatán Peninsula. Moving northward over the southern Gulf of Mexico on the 12th, it rapidly intensified from a Category 1 to a Category 4.

Third: formed on August 26, east of the Turks and Caicos Islands. It headed north-northwest while affecting the Turks and Caicos Islands and the Bahamas. It made landfall in South Florida on August 30.

Fourth: a rare Category 5 hurricane formed as a minimal tropical storm east of Puerto Rico on August 30.

Fifth: formed on September 9 in the southwest Gulf of Mexico. It headed northeast, strengthened and made landfall in Northwest Florida on September 15.

Sixth: formed on September 18 in the southwest Gulf of Mexico. It headed northeast, maintained strength, and made landfall near Marsh Island, Louisiana, on September 19, and continued farther inland into the United States.

Seventh: a tropical storm that was first observed east of the Lesser Antilles on September 25 rapidly intensified as it moved westward, reaching a peak of 120 mph (190 km/h) winds the next day.

Eighth: tropical storm formed on October 7 in the central Caribbean Sea northeast of Honduras. It headed northwest, and made landfall in northern Honduras on October 10. It then emerged into the southern Gulf of Mexico on October 12. It continued westward and eventually turned north and made landfall in Louisiana on October 15. It weakened to tropical depression status on October 16 in central Alabama, before dissipating on September 21 over southwestern West Virginia.

Ninth: a tropical storm formed on October 8 in the Atlantic Ocean northeast of the Virgin Islands. It headed northwest and got very close to Bermuda on October 10. It then turned northeast, was downgraded to a tropical depression and dissipated on October 12.

Tenth: tropical storm formed on October 30 in the Atlantic Ocean east of the Virgin Islands. It was upgraded to hurricane strength on November 1 as it headed southwest into the Caribbean Sea.

Eleventh: tropical storm formed on November 3 in the central Atlantic Ocean. It headed north into the Atlantic waters. It gained hurricane status on November 17 and turned northwest. As it continued, it strengthened to a peak of 100 mph (160 km/h), before weakening to an extra tropical storm on November 10, as it impacted the Azores.

Eleven storms in seven months. None of them said they made landfall in Lincoln. Mr. Kramer seemed to believe that conception had taken place in Lincoln. Yet, Mrs. Kramer, his mother, had conceived sometime during the storms of 1932. She could have been anywhere the storms hit. And if she was, that means other women in those places could have conceived, as well. Only I don't know for sure if Eleanor Kramer had a baby with powers. I so badly want to read the rest of that diary. Giving Jake the courtesy is killing me.

Beep. Beep.

The chirping startles me and I jump in my chair. Frowning, I realize it is just the instant messaging notifier on my computer.

I click the smiley-face icon and wait while the message appears in the small box.

To: krystalgem, princesssasha
From: ladieslovej
Found note n bk—re Salem Witch Trials???

It is Jake. Yeah, I know the screen name is laughable considering the owner. We'd exchanged cell phone numbers and ChicTeen chat room screen names before leaving Jake's house. Still I read the message again, further intrigued by Eleanor Kramer and what else she'd written in that diary.

Reply to: ladieslovej, princesssasha
From: krystalgem
U think we r witches?

Drumming my fingers on my desk, I wait for a reply, thoughts of witches burning at the stake on my mind.

Reply to: krystalgem, ladieslovej
From: princesssasha
OMG! Lk bg nose grn face witches?

Sasha is so dramatic.

Reply to: princesssasha, krystalgem
From: ladieslovej
No gt a grip. Only 1 letter about witches
Will look 4 more n am. Go 2 bd!

I can just see Jake frowning, looking at me and Sasha and wondering why we are on the computer at this time of night in the first place. But then again, he is online, too.

Anyway, we do have school tomorrow so I guess I should at least get into bed and try to sleep. Witches and hurricanes will certainly be there for us to investigate in the morning. I close down the windows with the weather research and am about to close out of ChicTeen when another IM pops up.

To: krystalgem
From: number1
C u 2morow

For seconds I just stare at the screen trying to remember if I know who "number1" is. I figured when Jake said he was registered that Sasha would be, too. This would be a way we could talk without anyone overhearing us and without running up our cell phone bills—for those who didn't have unlimited texting like me.

Then it hits me. It's this goofball again. I don't know who it is. I'd thought about it some more after the first message the other night. But if they're saying they'll see me tomorrow I guess it's someone here in Lincoln. In the profiles section you can put where you live. I know about putting too much of your personal info on the Net so at first I just had NYC. Then when I moved here I changed it to CT. Hoping that was vague enough. Apparently not. Still, I am convinced that whoever this "number1" is they don't really know who I am. I'm not exactly popular at Settlemans High.

With a shrug I just type "OK" real quick then exit out of the chat room and close down my computer. Climbing into bed feels like a monumentous task. I guess because so much happened today.

I'd seen three ghosts—Ricky, Trina and crying girl. Ricky, I'm not afraid of. Trina, I can tell is going to be a pain in the butt. But crying girl, she still has me wondering what I am really getting myself into. I wonder if she'll come back, call to me like Ricky had or just tell me what she wants. She didn't act like she wanted my help, but the feeling we shared said she probably needed it.

fourteen

"krystal, you're going to talk to Franklin about the weather stuff, right?" Jake asks, taking a bite of the sandwich he picked up while in the lunch line.

It looks like it could be some type of barbecued meat, but it's making my stomach churn as it falls off the bread and Jake hurriedly scoops it up and stuffs it into his mouth.

I take a sip of my soda and keep my fingers wrapped tightly around the cool can even when I set it back down on the table. "Yeah, I guess so." I shrug. "I don't really know how to approach this subject with him without telling him why I want to know. I mean, how's he supposed to know about weather patterns from sixteen years ago, let alone eighty years ago?"

"He won't," Jake says even though his mouth is full and it sounds more like "re ront." His eyes roll in his head as he tries to hurry and chew then talk. "But his father's the weatherman. They've lived in Lincoln forever. I'm sure he probably knows something."

"Okay, and what am I supposed to say when he asks me why I want to know?"

Sasha sighs. "Don't say anything. I mean, don't go to him asking questions like you're working on a school paper or something. Just kind of talk to him. I saw how he was all goo-goo eyed at you the other day so just play that role and I'm sure he'll tell you anything."

She's wearing low-ride jeans today and a cropped graphic T-shirt that's fuchsia and black. The design has fuchsia glitter on the front and she's wearing long, dangly fuchsia feather earrings. I suspect it's because of her pink *M* that we discovered last night and that nobody else can see because it's not glowing now.

Before leaving Jake's house last night, after Mr. Kramer had gone into the other room to settle into the old worn recliner with a bowl of chips and a diet Coke to watch *Jeopardy,* we decided this power would be our secret.

I'm wearing a short-sleeved shirt, a button-down light blue top—yeah, apparently I was feeling the same way Sasha was this morning, although I hate to admit it. Around my neck I have a blue choker-style necklace because while I'm starting to feel okay with this power thing, I'm still a little leery about everybody seeing my *M*.

Jake has on his usual, a T-shirt with a hoodie over top of it, so seeing his mark is out of the question. And he's not wearing green clothes, apparently the idea of being color coordinated with the mark didn't quite reach him.

"Play what role?" I ask, finally letting Sasha's words sink in.

"You know what role. Like you're interested in him the way he is in you. Like you want to get with him."

"But I don't want to get with him," I say real quick and then wonder why the words tumbled out so fast.

Sasha smirks. "You sure? 'Cause I saw him at your locker this morning and you were smiling."

Okay, she has me there. I was smiling this morning when Franklin did his imitation of Martin Lawrence in *Welcome Home, Roscoe Jenkins*. Apparently it was on cable last night. Franklin asked me had I watched it and I'd just shrugged and said no. I couldn't exactly tell him that instead I'd been experiencing a mini-heatstroke in Jake's bedroom while our birthmarks glowed like lightning bugs.

"We were talking about a movie," I say in my defense.

"Whatever. He likes you and whether or not you like him—which by the way I think you do—just go with it. Get the info we need so we can move on."

"And where are we moving on to?" I ask, praying this will get us off the topic of Franklin and whether or not I like him. "I mean, what are we going to do about this...this thing between us?"

"You mean this power," Jake says with his head down again. At first he was talking loud and a lot then suddenly, when Sasha started talking about me and Franklin, he'd put his head down and focused more on his sandwich.

"Yeah, I mean this power." It still sounded strange to just admit that all of us had power as plainly as saying all of us had acne—which, by the way, Sasha and I didn't. I noticed that Jake had a few zits under that long flap of hair he kept over his forehead. Maybe that's why he kept the hair there in the first place.

"We use it," Sasha answers simply. Like me and Jake are ignorant and she is the only one with an ounce of sense. That fact I definitely beg to differ with but I don't say anything.

"To do what?" I ask instead.

Sasha sticks her last celery stick into her mouth and balls up the plastic bag she'd been taking them from. Lifting her bottled water to her lips, she drinks till its gone, then puts the empty bottle into the brown paper bag along with the plastic bag from the celery and balls it up, too.

"We start by helping Ricky Watson figure out what happened to him. See, ever since you said you saw him I've been reading about ghosts. And sometimes they do need help crossing over. Ricky must feel like there's something he needs to do first to be free to walk over to the other side. So we have to help him figure out what that is and get his soul to moving where it belongs."

I take another sip of soda and mull over her words. She's right, I know, because I thought it myself. Ricky isn't going away until I—I guess now that will be *we*—help him. "In your reading did it say another spirit could help him get to the other side?" I ask, thinking about Trina.

Sasha nods quickly. "No. Not if the reason he's not moving on is rooted here in the living world. Somebody living has to help him. Somebody who can hear and/or see him so he can tell them what to do."

"And that somebody is you," Jake says quietly. "You're the medium, the link between the spirit world and the living."

I sort of already figured that out. "Okay, so what else did the diary say? Anything that can tell us why we are what we are?"

Jake shrugs. "I stopped reading right after she had the baby. A boy, my grandpa's older brother. So far there's nothing strange or powerful about him."

"Keep reading," Sasha says. "I've got a feeling there's answers for us in there."

For what might be the first time, I have to agree with her.

"Hey, Krystal, since you can see and talk to the dead, you think you could call the dead?" Sasha asks, propping her elbows up on the table, her hazel eyes just about glittering as she watches me expectantly.

"No!" My voice gets a little higher. I look around but nobody notices. "I'm not calling the dead. Besides I don't think I can. I think they just come to me, you know, with stuff they want to say."

"You mean you've heard them before Ricky?" Sasha scoots up closer to the table and stares at me.

Jake is looking at me, too, and I feel like I'm one of those animals at the zoo that nobody has ever heard of so people stand in front of the cage and stare at all stupidly.

"Yes, I've heard them before," I say but don't look away. Because in this case, Sasha with her disappearing acts and Jake with his Incredible Hulk strength are just as weird and unheard-of as me.

Sasha's eyes get bigger, like what I'm saying is really exciting her. "So what else have they said to you?"

"Just stuff, I guess. I mean, I never really paid attention until Ricky. The other times I just kind of put it out of my mind, convinced myself that I couldn't hear it and moved on. Eventually it stopped." Only now I'm afraid that since I acknowledged Ricky I've opened the floodgates.

"But Ricky didn't," Jake says, looking up at me.

"No." I shake my head. "Ricky didn't."

"Right, because he needs your help really bad. He needs our help," Sasha says with what seems like too much conviction.

Almost immediately Jake reaches into his notebook and pulls out a sheet of paper. "I think I found out the meaning of our birthmarks," he says slowly, placing the paper in the middle of the table.

Both Sasha and I look down at it. I scrunch up my face because it looks kind of cryptic, like the writing is upside down. Jakes uses his finger to slide the sheet of paper closer to us, and I realize it's a drawing of the *M* on his arm that I drew last night—the mark we all share. The only difference is he's written some other letters below the *M* now so that it looks like some kind of logo. The other letters are *Y S T Y X*.

"My sticks?" Sasha asks, her face contorted in an expression that clearly reflects her confusion.

Jake shakes his head. "I was flipping through the journal last night and saw this word scribbled in the margins on a couple of pages. MYSTYX. I didn't know what it meant so I checked it on Google and came up with notes about the River Styx."

"The river between Earth and the Underworld," I say, remembering this little tidbit from Greek mythology.

He smiles. "Right!"

"Greeks? Underworld? Are you two cracking up? Maybe we were up just a little too late last night," Sasha replies.

"No," Jake says, shaking his head while he talks. "It kind of makes sense. Listen, in Greek mythology the River Styx was viewed by the gods as having miraculous powers."

"So you think our powers come from a mythical river?" Sasha asks.

I have to admit it does sound crazy and almost unbelievable. But then again, so does the fact that I can see and talk to ghosts and Sasha can disappear and Jake is super strong. There is a part of me that is open to the idea and seems to understand the connection.

"I think it's a part of who and why we are. I don't know exactly how yet, but I can feel that it's a key to our being," said Jake.

Sasha is the one nodding while Jake's still talking, as if she's trying to align her thinking with us.

I look over at her and catch her eye. I nod and slowly repeat, "My Styx. My river. My power."

Then Jake jumps in. "But it's pronounced like mystics because to us mere mortals," he adds in a tone that I guess is supposed to be his otherworldly voice, "the Power would be considered more mystical than godlike."

Now Sasha's smiling. "Cool. We're the Mystyx, our own little clique that nobody can join or enter because they have to have the Power, too."

"You think there are others that have the Power?" I ask, remembering the storms reported in 1932 and that they were in all different places.

"There's gotta be. I mean, what are the odds that only three women were pregnant in Lincoln at the same time?"

Jake frowns. "Well, considering there are only a couple thousand people in Lincoln altogether, the odds are pretty good."

"Well, it doesn't matter. We're here, right now, and we know we have the Power. And now we have a reason for using that Power. We're ready to save the world!"

She's all animated, looking like she's auditioning for a school play. I have to admit her words make me feel kind of special, like there is something that only I can do to help someone. And it doesn't matter that my parents are no longer together or that my stepfather is a mean bastard or that the spirit that wants my help has a girlfriend. All that matters is that we are here, with this Power, with this job to do. Like Jake said, we are the Mystyx.

Then another thought hits me. "I'm not wearing a costume or a cap and stockings."

For one awkward second our table is quiet then one by one we all start to laugh.

The joke is short-lived because Alyssa and Camy stop at our table. Jake seems to hunker down a bit more, focusing once again on his food. Sasha perks up more, if that were possible, and smiles.

"Hey, Alyssa, Camy. What's up?"

While the two girls have been frowning at me, when they hear Sasha they both look at her and return her smile. Alyssa is a little shorter than me, probably somewhere around five feet two inches. I am tall for my age at five feet four inches, but the doctor said I am slowing down and would probably top out at five-six.

Today Alyssa's braids are pulled back in a loose bun with wisps hanging out the sides and down her back. Her mocha-toned skin looks perfect as do the sea-green eyes (so totally contacts). She's squeezed into a pair of jeans and an even tighter silver-and-white T-shirt. Beside her, the sidekick Camy is wearing some expensive jeans, I can't tell which ones because her long sweater vest is covering them. Camy's straw-blond hair is left long, hanging flawlessly past her shoulders. They look like two Barbie dolls. No, scratch that, they look like those big-eyed Bratz dolls, with big heads and lots of hair. It is a struggle for me not to giggle.

"Hi, Sasha. Please tell me there's a good reason for you to be sitting here with *her*."

That is Alyssa speaking, I think there is like this unspoken rule that she has to talk first before Camy can follow up. The way Alyssa tossed her head in my direction and spat the word *her* was something else to make me laugh. This girl took herself way too seriously.

"Oh? You know Krystal? I hadn't realized you two had met." To her credit, Sasha doesn't seem to fall into Alyssa's snobbish trap. Although she certainly could have considering she is a Richie just like Alyssa and Camy.

"She's in one of our classes," Camy adds with a roll of her eyes. "But really, you can find better lunch partners."

"I'm not begging anyone to sit here," I finally speak up, tired of them talking around me.

Sasha shoots me a look that I can't tell is wounded or irritated. You never can tell with Sasha, as moody as she is.

"I happen to like sitting here," Sasha says. "You want to join?" Then, without even looking at Alyssa, Sasha reaches into her purse, pulls out a lip gloss tube and proceeds to smear it on her lips.

"Ugh, please. I wouldn't be caught dead at a table with her."

There it is again, that special way Alyssa has of saying "her."

"Then be gone," I snap.

Camy, probably without permission to speak, simply

lifts her hand and forms an *L* shape with her fingers, pointing in my direction.

I take the last swallow of my soda and say, "Bite me."

"Digestion is not conducive to arguing, ladies," Sasha says. "Besides, the bell's about to ring."

And as if all things work at her command the bell does just that.

Scooping up my trash, I don't waste any time moving away from the table. Jake, who has been quiet during the exchange, is right behind me. Alyssa and Camy, who are too dumb to know when their intimidation tactics have totally failed, stand in my way, looking grim like Nazi police.

I guess they think they're scaring me. Well, I have news for them. I am receiving daily visits by dead people, these two pampered princesses don't stand a chance. I push past both of them, hard, hoping I'll knock one of them to the ground the way Ricky did the other day.

"You better watch your back, new girl." I hear Alyssa yell but don't bother to turn around.

I have other things to deal with besides her.

Out of the corner of my eye, I catch a glimpse of Ricky. He is sitting at the table where the other hip-hoppers sit. The other guys are there, too, but of course they can't see him. I wonder what they are saying, what, if any, information Ricky is getting from them.

Then I wonder why it matters so much.

fifteen

It is my job to talk to Franklin, but that will have to wait. Janet, true to her words from last night, shows up after school to take me to the shrink.

Sasha is going to talk to Antoine to see what she can find out about Ricky and what happened before he was killed.

Jake is going home to fix his grandfather dinner and to hopefully get some more information from him about this Power we all share. We all seem pretty cool with the fact that we have it and that it comes from some freak storm, but we want to know more. Like if there are more of us out there. I believe there are since bizarre weather could happen anywhere in the world, if that is the real cause. Sasha wants to find out really bad so we can build some type of network of Mystyx all over the world. She really does think big, which I guess is okay when you are rich and have everything. But the funny thing is that having everything doesn't seem to make Sasha too happy. I mean, she doesn't strike me as an Alyssa or Camy; money and status don't really seem to faze her one way or the other. Because if it does, she certainly wouldn't be hanging with Jake, or me for that matter.

This might be the tallest building I've seen in Lincoln. It

is on one of the main streets, right at the end of the block past the post office and pharmacy. Built with red brick and white trimmed windows, it looks both modern and old at the same time. It is five stories high and has a sign in the front lobby that states which office is on what floor.

My destination is floor number four.

Janet has been quiet on the ride over here and she is quiet now that it is just me and her in the elevator. I don't much care because I have a lot on my mind already. Trying to be polite and talking to her would just distract me.

She opens the door for me after we both stand in front of it for longer than is probably necessary. I wonder if she is changing her mind. I definitely would not have a problem with it if she is. But then she moves ahead and I have no choice but to follow her.

The nurse-receptionist lady is old, her face like cracked leather, her glasses sliding down her shiny nose. She isn't happy with her job, I surmise by the pinched look on her face. Either that or that fake bun on the back of her head is pinned on way too tight.

Bitter Lady (what I am now calling the nurse-receptionist because I don't know her name and she hasn't bothered to tell us) calls Janet's name and gives her some forms to fill out while I just sit there looking at this big-screen television with a never-ending infomercial on it. I can feel my cell phone vibrating and wonder if I should dare to answer it. Janet would not like the interruption and I might not like who is calling. Although I do need to talk to Franklin—if it is him—I can't do it in front of Janet.

Or it could be Daddy calling me back. Finally. But Janet won't like that either. By the time I finish debating, it stops vibrating and Janet never notices she is so busy writing on that clipboard.

The purse I carry is small compared to the other girls in school, compared to the large designer bag Sasha carries.

I can't figure out what she keeps in there, her entire bedroom probably. But I don't like all that clutter so I have a cute bag Janet bought for me the last Christmas we were all together as a family. It's black with silver fringe and has a long enough strap to criss-cross over my body. I don't like for it to swing off my arm. Anyway, my cell phone is in there. I'll dig it out later and see who the missed call was from.

Right now my name's being called by the Bitter Lady and I have to go see the whack quack so he can try to figure out what's wrong with me. I can answer that question in the first few seconds of our visit—nothing.

"So, Krystal, why don't you tell me about yourself?"

He starts talking the minute Janet leaves me in the room alone with him. Or should I say, the clock starts ticking. He doesn't think I notice but I can see the clock on his desk tilted so that only he can see it. Plus there are clocks all over his office.

One on the wall near the door, it is brown and matches the dull color of the sofa along the wall. There is another one on a small table near a recliner that may have been comfortable twenty or thirty years ago. And on one of the bookshelves that line the whole opposite wall, there is a small digital blaring the numbers 4:35 in bright red.

I sit in one of the chairs right across from his desk—oh, his name's Dr. Heathcliff Small. But his nose is huge—a definite contradiction to his name. I wonder if his mother had any idea when he was born.

"Don't you already know that stuff?" I ask, slouching in the chair. My mind is so not on this so-called doctor's visit, or cry for help that Janet believes this is. Instead I'm more worried about how Sasha's interrogation of Antoine is going.

More importantly, I'm wondering where Ricky's been hiding himself. Or, actually, who he's been hiding out with.

I mean, let's face it, for all I know he could have already found his way over to the other side and left me high and dry. That's usually what people in my life do.

"Do you like school?"

Dr. Whack Quack (I'm going to keep calling him that because that's what I think he is) is asking me another question. I guess to pass the time I might as well go ahead and answer him. I mean, really, I don't have to agree with being here but since I'm still under eighteen and since Janet seems to think this is the best course of action for me, I might as well go with the flow.

"School is okay."

"Do you have a favorite subject?"

I shrug. "Does anybody?"

He looks at me funny, like maybe he's getting tired of my teenage attitude. Well, I'm tired of his old-man shrink attitude.

"I like math, I guess."

"Are you passing all your classes?"

"Yes. I'm passing all my classes. I don't hook school, I do my homework. I turn in all my projects. I don't hang out late. I'm always in the house. I don't do drugs. I don't have friends who do drugs."

Then he holds up a hand as if to stop my monologue. I lift my brow, waiting for him to come up with another question because I could swear I've answered all the normal ones already.

"How about your home life? How do you feel about your mother's new husband?"

Well, okay, I guess I didn't anticipate that question, but since he put it out there we'll just hop right to it. "I don't have to like him. I'm not the one married to him."

"That's fair. However, I understand you've been through a kind of transition. How do you feel about that?"

"I feel like I'm fifteen. I don't really have a whole lot of choice in the matter. The adults call the shots. That's just the way it is. So for right now I have to listen."

"You don't sound too happy about that."

"What teenager would?"

"Let's try it this way. How do you feel about the breakup between your parents?"

That is probably the million-dollar question. How do I feel about Janet and my dad breaking up? How do I feel about being uprooted from the only life I've ever known, to come and live in this small town where Janet had grown up? More importantly, how do I feel about the fact that it has been almost a month and a half since I've spoken to my father and more than a dozen phone calls and voice mails to him are left unanswered? How is a fifteen-year-old supposed to feel about that?

"I don't really know," I answer him honestly.

"Are you angry?"

"No. I don't think so."

"Are you sad?"

"Not really. I mean, I was in the beginning but I'm really not now."

"Take a few minutes to think of a word that would best describe what you're feeling at this very moment."

"Disappointed," I say after only a few seconds.

"Disappointed in your mother?"

I nod yes.

"Disappointed in your father?"

I continue nodding.

"Disappointed in yourself?"

I pause for a minute and think about that one. Then I just shrug because I think he may be right.

"Let's start with your mother. Why are you disappointed with her?"

"Because I think she's a coward. She ran away instead of staying and trying to make things work between her and my dad."

"Did she tell you why she left?"

"No. And that's another reason why I think she's a coward. Why can't she just answer my questions?"

"Do you answer all the questions she asks you?"

Folding my arms over my chest, I look toward the bookcase he has on the side of the wall. There are a kazillion books piled onto it with titles that I don't understand.

"I wonder if you and your mother made an agreement to every day answer, honestly, at least one question each other has, if that would make you feel better."

"She won't do it."

"Will you?"

I look at my watch to see if our hour is almost over.

"What are your plans for the rest of the day?"

I turn back to stare at him, more than a little puzzled by the quick change of subject. I had thought since this was Janet's idea for me to come and talk to him she'd have this shrink on her side and he'd spend an entire hour telling me how wrong I am for not talking to her or for being upset with her. Instead, he's asking me about a whole bunch of other stuff that I really don't want to talk about either.

I really don't want to be here.

I just don't want to talk to him. Or anybody else for that matter.

Answering his questions makes me think and what I'm thinking isn't too cool.

sixteen

This really isn't a date.

A date is when a guy picks you up and takes you someplace like the movies or dinner.

I'm heading to the library to meet Franklin. I guess that could be like a study date, although I don't plan on studying.

I saw him in the hallway today and he asked if we could study together after school. I knew I needed to talk to him about the weather stuff so I agreed. But now, walking up the steps toward the heavy glass and brass doors of the public library, I begin to think it might be for some other reason.

My jeans are new, the skinny fit in dark denim, and my white T-shirt and hoodie matched the inseam threading as well as my white high-top sneakers. Coordinating my wardrobe had never been a big deal before. I guess hanging with Sasha is rubbing off. Or maybe I secretly want to look good for Franklin. A few nights ago I would have said Ricky, but I've since come to terms with my crush on the spirit that needs my help. Speaking of which, I haven't seen him in a minute and wonder what that means.

I am just about to walk through the library doors when I hear someone scream behind me. Stopping, I turn because now I'm tuned in to screams, yells, anything that projects fear, because I think it involves a ghost. So anyway, I turn but don't think it's a spirit that I'm seeing. Instead a group of younger kids are running, their arms waving in the air. Above their heads are three large birds, black birds like crows, I think.

Without hesitating I run down the steps and get in front of the children. I wave my taller, longer arms upward to shoo the birds away. The screeching grows louder and I think my wrist actually makes contact with one of them. At that moment it's like they shift and take aim at me.

"Get inside!" I yell to the kids and keep swatting at the nuisance birds trying to peck my eyes out.

From out of nowhere a heavy gust of wind rushes around the corner and past me. I stumble and fall flat on my face, my cheek kissing the asphalt. Above I still hear the screeching and with the fear of the birds pecking the hell out of the back of my head I hurriedly roll over.

The birds are still there, screeching, flying over me, but they are not alone. The wind is still blowing and a thick black cloud of smoke is rolling up from my feet to my waist. I try to scoot back out of its way but it just keeps coming, keeps trying to cover me.

There's a pounding in my chest and I feel like I can't breathe. The blackness is getting closer and closer; I feel like I'm dying.

Then I'm lifted into the air. Well, not exactly lifted, but my arms are pulled up so hard and my chest slams into another chest and I'm both dizzy from the movement and coughing from the cloud of dark smoke.

The cloud of smoke that, when I turn back around and look down, is gone.

* * *

"So what happened out there? Did you trip or something?" Franklin asks. We're sitting in the back of the library, near the "W" section of nonfiction.

We're sitting at a long table with chairs around both sides, but we're the only two people here. Franklin's chair is so close to mine they almost touch. Our legs are most definitely touching, his left one aligned neatly against my right one. That makes me feel tingly inside but not enough so that I can forget those stupid birds or that nasty black smoke. This is the third time I've seen it, the other two times in my dreams. I'm not really a believer in coincidences.

"Ah, yeah. There were these kids and they were running from some birds. I tried to help and I guess I fell." I finally answer Franklin because he's looking at me with eyes that I swear look like root beer soda.

My hands are flattened on the table and he puts one of his on top of one of mine. There is a slight contrast in our complexions but I have to say our hands look good together. Especially when he flips mine over and entwines our fingers.

"I didn't know what to think when I saw you lying on the ground."

"Probably that I was a lunatic," I say, only half joking.

He shakes his head. "No. I was worried that you were really hurt."

Wow, he was worried about me.

"I'm fine. Just a mishap, no big deal."

"Good," he says. "I've been wanting to spend some time with you for a while now."

"Really?"

"Yeah. Since you first started at Settlemans. I've been trying to think of a way to approach you because you don't seem like all the other girls here."

"Why? Because I'm not a Richie or a Tracker?"

He chuckles. "I don't go by those status codes. It's stupid and most of the people who follow them are, too."

"I agree," I answer, thinking that I am liking Franklin more and more.

Apparently my feelings are known to others as down at the other end of the table Ricky appears. He lounges back in the chair, arms crossed over his chest, giving me and Franklin a knowing smirk.

"So, you think you'll start accepting my calls now?"

I hear Franklin talking but I'm still looking at Ricky. Then Franklin waves his hand in front of my face.

"Krystal? Did you hear me?"

"Huh? Oh, yeah, I'm sorry. Just dazed off for a minute. Of course I'm going to take your calls. I've just been kind of tied up lately."

"Oh really? Is it schoolwork? 'Cause I can help you study if you want." Then the corner of his mouth lifts in a smile. "I mean, really study."

Because what we're doing now is definitely not studying. He's holding my hand, his other arm draped around the back of my chair and we're chatting like a boyfriend and girlfriend stealing time in the back of the library.

"Thanks, but it's not schoolwork." And then I figure that since Ricky has decided to invade my nice private moment with Franklin I might as well get down to business.

"I was just wondering what you thought about all this rain. It seems like it's forever raining here in Lincoln." That was true, in fact, it had rained earlier this morning.

He shrugs. "El Niño."

"Really? That's all you think it is, some strange weather system that blows through town every once in a while?"

"Yeah, that's what my dad says. He's at the station reporting on the heavy rains now."

"Hey, can you remember any other strange storms in Lincoln? I mean like a few years back." I didn't want to say sixteen years back to be specific especially considering he would have been a newborn then.

"We have storms and stuff all the time. Sometimes they're worse than others. I do remember a really big rainstorm a few years back and some flooding. And my dad talks about all the storms when he was young."

"I bet he saw a lot of, like, blizzards and stuff, too." Ricky's still sitting there, lifting his arms as if to say, "What are you doing?" I quickly look away from him.

"He talks about them all the time. I mean, like every time the weather changes again. He even has this system that helps him predict some of the bigger storms."

That gets all my attention. I lean in a little closer to Franklin, my eyes drift down for a second to the cute cleft in his chin, then back up to his eyes. *Very cute,* I think absently.

"A system, huh? That's funny because I thought I heard one of my mom's friends talking about a storm coming. Your dad thinking like that, too?"

"As a matter of fact, he did say he thought we were in for another one sometime soon."

It's then that Franklin reaches out a hand and touches my cheek.

"You're really pretty, Krystal," he says and all talk about weather flees my mind.

"I am?"

"You are."

He's leaning in closer and I don't know what to do. Ricky's watching. I want Franklin to kiss me, I think. But Ricky's watching. Did I want Ricky to kiss me, too? I used to, but he's a ghost, making that totally impossible and slightly insane.

My cell phone chimes and Franklin leans back.

Saved by the bell, my mind roars while my body has some regret-like reaction.

"Sorry," I mumble, reaching into my purse to get the phone. Pressing the button, I see the text and instantly feel nauseous.

seventeen

I am in my room now after having left Franklin and Ricky at the library. The text I received freaked me out and I needed to be alone. Only something tells me that I'm not.

Ignoring that feeling when I pull the cell phone out again, I scroll down until I find the text message and read.

Im a great photographer.
Will u pose 4 me?

As if that's not creepy enough, scrolling down a little further the picture reveals itself. The picture of a very alive, very naked Trina.

This whole situation just got a little more bizarre.

What kind of sick, perverted mess have I gotten myself involved in? Here I think I am helping out a spirit, doing something with the power I've been given, then another spirit comes along. A cute, street-wise, hot-to-trot spirit that I now know is into posing nude.

Yuck!

And whoever took this picture of her now wants to take pictures of me.

Double yuck!

There is no number so I don't know who the sender is. I guess if I call our cell phone provider I can find out. But then I'd have to tell Janet and she'd most definitely tell Gerald and I have no idea what he would do. Would he blame me? Would he punish me?

Where Gerald is concerned I just don't know.

So the obvious move would be to keep my mouth shut. I don't have to answer this text and I don't have to keep looking at it. But I don't delete it either.

No, I am going to wait for Ms. Trina to make another appearance, acting like she knows me on a personal level, telling me what I should do for her boyfriend. And then I'm going to pull out my phone, show her this pic and see what she has to say. Bet she won't act so high and mighty then.

The tapping wakes me up.

It sounds like a nail against the window but when I climb out of my bed to investigate, there is nothing there. I get back into bed, pull up the covers and burrow down to fall asleep again.

Screeeeeaaacccchhhhh!

Every nerve I have goes on end. My entire body stiffens as if keeping still will stop the god-awful sound. I cover my ears but it persists. Rolling over until I am flat on my back, I open my eyes wide to the darkness. Of course I see nothing, but it isn't what I can see that frightens me. It is the unknown.

Somebody or something is in the room with me. I can feel it, as easily as I feel my heart about to beat right out of my chest.

"Ricky?" I whisper his name but even as it falls off my lips I know it's not him. The feeling is not the same. My insides aren't fluttering around. Instead I'm breathing heavy, my chest has a dull ache in the center and my forehead is pounding. Whoever or whatever is here is not welcome.

But I don't think that's going to make them go away any sooner.

I sit up in the bed, despite the warning bells going off in my head and the little voice saying, "Don't be like those kids in the movies, you know the ones who always die first!" I push the covers off me thinking that's just fiction when my stuffed animal army comes barreling at me one by one, each smashing into my head, chest and arms with brutal force. As I raise my arms to ward them off, I can still hear that high-pitched screeching sound and wonder how long it's going to take for Janet to barge in here asking what's going on.

But after a few more seconds pass and, thankfully, all the stuffed animals have already been hurled at me, I figure that's not going to happen. So, putting my arms down I climb out of bed slowly, not knowing where I'm going or what I'm going to do when I get there. All I know for sure is that this is my room and there's no way I'm going to let some spiritual being or ghost or whatever keep me hostage in my bed. My feet touch the floor and I take the first step. It's quiet now, maybe the ghost or whoever had the wrong house.

A gust of wind has my nightgown whipping up my legs. As I'm struggling to pull it down my legs are hit with freezing cold air. Now I'm getting pissed off. I'm cold and I'm shivering and I'm trying to move toward the window that I now see is open. I know it wasn't open when I went to it just a few minutes ago. Then again, I also know that stuffed animals can't throw themselves across the room, no matter how much I dislike them.

Reaching out a hand, I try to grab hold of the edge of my dresser because this wind is crazy and in a minute I'm going to go flying through the air like my name should be

Dorothy and there should be a little barking dog beside me. But before my hand can grab the edge I'm stunned by the lifting of a charcoal pencil—one of the ones that Janet bought me the other day that I'd thrown on my floor. It floats toward the mirror and begins writing.

Still shivering, I'm standing in the middle of my room reading as the pencil writes *Charlotte Ethersby.*

The pencil falls to the dresser and rolls right off the end to the floor. By now I've crossed my arms. My teeth are chattering and my knees knocking.

"If you had something to say to me, Ricky, you could have just opened your mouth and said it. All this isn't necessary." I am so hoping it is him. Who else would come into my room in the middle of the night to leave me a cryptic message? It has to be Ricky, right?

Wrong.

The army of stuffed animals assault me again as they all circle around my feet until, as I'm busily trying to step over and around them, I fall to the floor with a loud thump. Then something falls on top of me. I can feel the weight but I can't see anything or anyone. What I do feel is the sharp pinch on my right cheek, the pinch that I soon realize is something scratching me.

To hell with this. I open my mouth and scream like somebody is attacking me. Which, by the way, they are. It just so happens to be a dead and invisible someone.

My screaming goes on forever and the weight on me finally shifts. I roll real quick, coming up on my knees, still trying to see something in the dark. Behind me the window slams shut and the breeze abruptly stops. The stuffed animals stay on the floor as evidenced by the one I trip over when I finally stand up and make my way across the room to my lamp. Flicking it on, I turn slowly to look around me, hating what I know I'm going to see.

Nobody.

That hard wind has blown papers from my desk all over the room, the stuffed animals are on the floor and so are all of the charcoal pencils from my dresser. The note on the mirror is there, visible and with some sort of meaning.

And there is something else.

On the floor right next to the window seat is a picture. I walk over, crouch down and pick it up. It was here, the crying girl spirit I'd seen at the school.

CYBER PREDATORS INVADE LINCOLN

Investigators in the Computer Crimes as well as Sexual Assault section of the Lincoln Police Department are looking into numerous claims of online sexual assault and sexting (text messages filled with sexual innuendo).

At the time of this report, three teenage girls in the area reportedly told their parents of mysterious text messages and instant messages received from an unknown source. The girls reported these actions after they thought they were being followed. The police have seized the computers and cell phones from these individuals and an investigation has begun.

Evening Headline
The Lincoln Gazette

eighteen

DID I ever mention that I hate Biology?

Well, I do.

It's one of those subjects that if you miss a day or two of work you are totally lost, which equals totally busted when quiz day arrives.

The fact that today's quiz is open book doesn't even help me. So for the first ten minutes I just stare at the work sheet, my mind more focused on what I had heard on the news this morning. Other girls were receiving texts and IMs of a sexual nature. I'd immediately thought about the messages I'd been receiving from "number1." I don't think I can say the IMs were sexual. Creepy, yes. But not really sexual. Now as for the text message, well, the naked picture definitely said sex. Did that mean the sender was hinting at having sex with me? He'd only mentioned posing for pictures. Had the person had sex with Trina? Maybe that's how she died.

I'm so full of questions it's no wonder I can't focus on schoolwork. But I don't have a choice. I either need to get it together or fail.

That's a no-brainer.

Finally, sighing wearily, I pick up my pen and open my

notebook. Flipping to the Biology section, I'm pleased to see that I do have the answers to the first ten questions in my notes. It's the other twenty that I'm having problems with. I'm trying to think back, maybe I heard Mr. Lyle talk about some of this stuff but just didn't write it down. I'm in deep concentration mode when the room gets a little darker. The sun must have shifted behind a cloud. I keep working.

The rain comes fast slapping against the window like a thousand tapping nails. I'm happy that when I look to the windows I'm not the only one. The entire class hears and sees the same thing. A sudden torrential rain doesn't seem to bother them though; they go right back to work.

Screaaacchhhhh!

The sound moves through my body tortuously slowly and I drop my pen. Bending down, I pick it up and on the way back up I hear the sound again. My eyes shoot around the classroom; everybody's still working. I look up front. Mr. Lyle is at his desk, looking down at something. Then I stifle a gasp. On the blackboard just behind Mr. Lyle the chalk is moving by itself.

It's scribbling across the board just like that charcoal had on my mirror last night.

MONEY. PICTURES. LIES. KILL.

I can't make myself stop looking. The room's still kind of dim, rain—actually it sounds more like hail now—slaps against the window. Then comes the breeze whirling around the room ruffling the pages in my notebook. The words on the blackboard repeat in swirly handwriting. By this point my heart's beating a frantic beat. I've gotta get out of here.

Slamming my notebook shut, I scoop it up in my arms and stand to leave. Nobody around me even looks up, like

I'm not even here. I'm moving fast heading to the door. I wonder if I need to get a hall pass. I look over at Mr. Lyle; he hasn't even looked up. So I keep moving until I brush past Mr. Lyle's desk, knocking over some papers. I hurry to pick them up and release a little yelp when I see writing on one of them.

MONEY. PICTURES. LIES. KILL.

Dropping them, I run straight to the door and out into the hall. I don't stop until I'm in the bathroom leaning over the sink, trying to catch my breath. From the speaker above I hear the bell ring and I close my eyes.

Apparently spirits are not the only things I see.

By lunchtime Sasha is even more wound up then she was this morning. I've had two more class periods to get myself together after the last ghostly encounter. I have no idea what the words meant but know that all of this is connected somehow.

Sasha's not eating her lunch and she keeps twirling strands of her hair around her finger. She looks like her mind is someplace else even though she's sitting right at the table talking to me and Jake. I think about asking her what's really wrong but then I stop. Sasha and I are too different to be friends. We're just Mystyx.

"What happened to your face?" she asks while I'm opening up the sandwich Janet packed for me. I know it's ham, cheese and mustard on whole wheat because that's what she gives me every day. I usually don't even bother to open it since I have no intention of eating it. Today, though, I'm hungry.

Dropping the sandwich, I immediately lift my hand to my right cheek. I'd seen the scratch this morning as I looked in the mirror after my shower. It had come from my evening visitor.

I wonder if I should tell them about that and the text and the vision I had in class this morning, but then I decide against it. I don't know how Trina's involved or who Charlotte Ethersby is, so I don't know what we need to do for Ricky. And he hasn't reappeared so I can ask him.

"It's nothing. I fell."

"Did you talk to Franklin?" she follows up.

The mention of his name has me looking around the cafeteria to see if he's there. I don't see him. "Yeah, I did. He says his father has a system to track weather patterns and that he thinks there's a big storm brewing."

"Really?" Jake says. "That's interesting."

"Why's it interesting? I could have turned on the television to get that very same report. Doesn't really help us either way."

Jeez. She was in a snippy mood today.

"But it might," Jake begins, scooting up closer to the table and putting down the magazine he was only pretending to read. Inside the magazine was the diary of Eleanor Jean Kramer. "Listen to this. December 1946—"

"Wait, the diary started in 1932. There aren't that many pages but it goes..." Sasha counts off to herself. "It goes fifteen years."

"She doesn't write consistently," Jake says, sounding a little irritated at Sasha's interruption.

"'William's doing things. Strange things. If he looks at something it moves. No matter what it is, all he has to do is look at it, focus on it and it moves. He's confused. I want to help him but I am afraid. Afraid of the darkness.'"

Sasha perks up. "What darkness?"

Jake shrugs. "It stops right there."

"Darkness," I begin talking, picturing it clearly in my mind. "The dark fog. I saw it."

"What?" they both ask in unison.

Then just Jake. "What did you see and when?"

"Yesterday when I fell, there was this black fog all around me. It kept moving and moving like it was going to choke me."

"Did it say anything?" Sasha asks.

"No. It was a fog. Not a spirit. It didn't speak or anything, just kept coming."

"That doesn't sound good," Jake says.

"No. It doesn't."

For a few minutes we're all quiet, not really knowing what to say next.

"How did it go with Antoine?" Jake asks suddenly.

Sasha frowns. "He's a jerk."

And she says it with an attitude that makes both Jake and I look at each other in question then back at her.

"And?" he says.

"And he was an even bigger jerk when I asked about his brother. He was like, 'Yo, that's in the past. I'm tryna make a future wit me and you. What you tryna do?'"

I chuckle. Can't help it, her imitation of the thug-lovin' Antoine Watson is right on point. I know because I over-heard him talking to his friends this morning by the gym.

Jake smiles, too. "So he tried to get with you instead of helping you? Is that what's got you so ticked off?"

Sasha rolls her eyes at both of us. "I'm not ticked off."

Jake nods and I go back to unwrapping my sandwich. She is lying and not doing a good job of it.

"So did you find out anything that could help us?"

Sasha huffs so hard her bangs flip up and fall back down in spiral ringlets on her forehead. "Just that Ricky was dating this girl Trina before she turned up missing. A few people said Ricky did something to her. Said they had a fight over money or something."

"Money?" Jake whispers.

I am remaining quiet, waiting to hear what else she has to say, wondering how it will relate to the picture on my phone or the message on the blackboard.

"He said it was more like Ricky was hounding Trina about where she was getting all this money. Trina told him to mind his business, got mad and broke up with him."

Jake looks like he is processing the information, too. "And what, she killed him?"

Sasha shakes her head. "Nope. Antoine said Trina went missing before Ricky died. Somebody saw them fighting and then Trina was gone."

"Gone like dead?"

Sasha shrugs. "Gone like gone. I don't know. That's all I could get from him before he started getting too close."

I take a bite of my sandwich and let the food move around in my mouth for a few seconds before attempting to swallow. I wonder if it'd threaten to get stuck like that pizza did. But as I continue to chew and breathe it doesn't, it just slides down my throat like it is supposed to.

"Gone like dead," I say when the food is finally down and I don't feel like it's going to come back up.

I can feel their stares on me and reluctantly look up. Accepting it, waiting for the onslaught of questions that will follow.

"How do you know?"

"Have you seen her, too?"

"Did Ricky kill her?"

I hate when they tag-team question me. "Yeah, I saw her. I don't think he killed her." Then again, I don't know. I don't know much about Ricky or his girlfriend.

What I do know is that I want to talk to Ricky again, to ask him some of these questions for myself.

"So what else happened that has you so ticked off with Twan?" I change the subject.

A neatly arched brow lifts. "Twan?"

I shrug. "That's what Ricky calls him."

Sasha rolls her eyes sideways, determined not to look at me. Or Jake either, for that matter. Instead she glances over to the table where Twan is sitting. Something is definitely going on there, something I am sure she isn't going to be up front about. Which is probably okay considering all the little tidbits of info I'm keeping from them.

"They're just a callous bunch of thugs. They don't care who they hurt."

"Did he hurt you?" I ask. Concern for Sasha is quick, natural and new to me.

She shakes her head. "No. Not me. Not him. I just mean I didn't really feel comfortable being with him. I mean, with that group."

I have no idea what she's talking about. I guess I sort of get what she's saying but she's being rather cryptic. I open my mouth to say something else but Jake shakes his head as if warning me to let it go.

"Well, Ricky was definitely down with them. For how long and what role did he play with them?" Jake asks.

Sasha hunches her shoulders. "I don't know. Like I said, he wasn't really into giving me a lot of information about Ricky. More like trying to get in my pants. The creep!"

So that's what has her all out of sorts. Twan was trying to get with her instead of giving information. I almost repeat what she told me yesterday about going along and playing like I want to get with Franklin the way he wants to get with me. But I stop and ask myself why a girl who looks like Sasha, with long pretty hair, pretty eyes, the stylish clothes and the curvy little figure, isn't automatically pleased with the fact that yet another guy is trying to get with her. Then it hits me. A girl like Sasha—a Richie—and a boy like Twan, a hip-hopper who probably gets into more trouble than he gets good grades. Only I don't think Sasha is into all that social status stuff.

"What I do know is that they're not, like, a gang or anything. Just a group of guys who grew up together and stick together because nobody understands them. That's what Antoine says. You'd just think they'd grow up and start doing something more useful with their time." Then she turns, her eyes perking up just a bit. "I also know they have something deep to talk about tomorrow night."

"Deep? Like what?" Jake asks.

"Tomorrow night he said they're going to meet in the music room during basketball practice. I only got that info from him when he was trying to figure out what night I'd be available to spend with him. He quickly ruled that out."

"Cool." Jake is nodding his head. "I say we should definitely be there."

Sasha and I both look at him quizzically.

"What?"

"We should be there. Find out what's so important, what's going on with them. The only way we're going to get close to what may have happened to Ricky is to get close to those he was tight with."

"Has he given you any details about his death?"

I shake my head no because in the two weeks that Ricky's been asking for my help, he's yet to actually tell me about his murder. And for the first time in those two weeks, I'm thinking how strange that is.

"We haven't really talked about that."

Tilting her head, Sasha glares at me. "What do you mean, you haven't talked about that? You've been talking to a ghost, he asks you for your help but you haven't talked about his death? What do you two talk about?"

Okay, first of all I really don't think it's any of her business what I talk about with anybody, living or dead, besides her and Jake. Still I get the idea of why she asked and I see where she's going with the conversation. It's not making me very comfortable—then again, being around Sasha usually doesn't.

"We just talk about stuff," I say, knowing that's not going to be enough. So I instantly take a deep follow-up breath and prepare to go into that "stuff" a little further.

"Okay, look, we're all in this together so any information you've got about your little ghost friend, his club, his death, whatever, spill."

Drumming my fingers on the table, I simply shake my head. Sometimes this girl really irks me. "After I first accepted that I was actually talking to a spirit, we just kind of talked about basic stuff. Who he is, what his problem is. You know, stuff like that."

"And that's all?" Skeptical should have been her middle name. "How many times have you and he talked about just basic stuff?"

"Just a couple."

Then I think about my dream where I woke up in the cemetery right next to Ricky's tombstone and I wonder if that has any importance on what we're doing. "I know where he's buried," I blurt without thinking.

"Well, yeah, there's only one cemetery in Lincoln," Sasha informs me.

Then Jake chimes in, "You've been to the cemetery to see his grave?"

I shake my head. "It was in my dream. I ah—" Not really wanting to go into the part of the dream where I'm reliving the way my mother snatched me from New York and dropped me here, I stall for a few seconds. "It's like I'm running, either from something or toward something. I never figure it out. And then I fall. When I get up I'm right in front of Ricky's grave. I try to get away and I run into…that same black fog," I say. "Like that's where I'm supposed to be and what I'm supposed to see. Odd."

"Not odd. Maybe it's just a clue."

I agree with Jake because it is safer to do so than to explain why I was having the whacky dream in the first place.

"You know how he died?"

"I think he was shot," Sasha says.

Jake nods. "Yeah. I think I remember something like that. They found his body in that alley behind the school."

"So he was shot here in school?"

"It was, like, after school hours so I don't really remember if he was shot during schooltime or what, but I think that's where they found his body."

"Do you think you could get more information? More clues to kind of figure out which direction we should be looking?" Sasha asks and I want to pick up on the sarcasm in her voice. I want to have a reason to snap back at her, but I really don't. Because in a way she is right. If I am the medium and we are supposed to be finding out what really happened to the spirit, then I should have more clues. After all, Jake and Sasha can't ask him what the hell happened. Only I can do that. And if I am going to be in this Mystyx thing for the long haul, I should definitely do my part. And I planned to do just that, only I don't think I have to tell them everything right at this minute. Aside from that, I usually just waited for Ricky to appear and start talking to me. I'm not sure if I can actually call him and talk to him, like if there is some sort of ghost GPS I can use to get in touch with him.

"I'll ask," I say finally. "And I'll get back to you guys."

Sasha nods. "We need some sort of meeting place."

"You mean like a clubhouse?" Jake asks.

"We're not elementary schoolers," Sasha says, rolling her eyes. Then as if she finally realizes how bitchy she's being today, Sasha takes a deep breath. Using her fingers she rubs her temples and puts her head down like she is just too through. I am so tempted to ask her what else is going on because in that moment I know there has to be something above and beyond this Mystyx thing or even the fact that a skuzzy guy was trying to get with her. I don't know how I know, I just do.

"We can meet at my house," she says. Her voice sounds all grumbly because her head's down on the table.

Now it's me and Jake's turn to just look at each other. Then I presume that he's too nervous to say something so I say it.

"What did you say?"

Sasha lifts her head slowly. "We can meet at my house. I mean, at my pool house. That way my parents won't be all in our business. Say, tonight around six-thirty. I've got somewhere to go right after school but I'll be back home by then."

Well, it is obvious that she isn't going to tell us where she has to go after school. And I guess I really shouldn't care. So I just shrug. "Sure, that sounds fine."

Jake asks, "You think you'll talk to Ricky by then?"

I don't know. Unlike what is called a necromancer, I don't have the power to actually wake or call the dead— or at least I don't think so. I just figure they can talk to me and I can hear them. But maybe…maybe if I go to Ricky's home (so to speak), knock on the door and ask for him, he'll appear. Huh, it can't be that easy.

Then again, maybe it isn't that hard.

nineteen

Dreaming about being in the cemetery is one thing. Actually purposefully creeping into the cemetery, walking past the different sized and designed headstones, searching for someone in particular, is a whole other realm of freakiness.

Lincoln Memorial Gardens is located a couple blocks from Main Street, right on the corner of the United Presbyterian Church. It's not as big as some cemeteries I've seen, but it's big enough. Walking through the cast-iron gates is a little different from the last time I think I was here. In the dream I'd just appeared in front of Ricky's grave. Now, I'll have to walk through the maze of headstones to find it.

Or do I?

I am already through the gates and heading in the direction I think I should start when I stop. I have the power to see, hear and communicate with spirits of the afterlife. Could there be something more? What if I could call to other beings, somehow communicate in their realm? Well, there is certainly no harm in trying.

Searching my mind for all the stuff I'd read online about mediums and the afterlife, I begin to relax myself. Standing perfectly still, I close my eyes and think about Ricky. He's the spirit I want to contact, the one I need to speak to, so I figure he should be the one to think about.

For endless moments I stand there in the fading sunlight and breezeless afternoon. Actually, it had looked a little cloudy as I'd approached the cemetery…but that is getting off track. I need to concentrate for this to work. I think.

I picture Ricky again, his chocolate-brown complexion and dark pensive eyes. I think about his long arms that more often than not are folded across his chest and those heavy boots he wears that never seem to be tied tightly. My heart stumbles as I hear his laughter as clearly as if he's standing right beside me. But I don't open my eyes to see if that's true, something inside tells me not to. To keep the link open and alive.

So I keep my breaths steady, in and out, in and out.

Krystal.

The sound of my name interrupts Ricky's laughter and then a soft breeze sweeps across my face. At my sides my fingers are clenching and unclenching. I want to run because the voice calling my name doesn't sound like Ricky. But again, something keeps me still, keeps my eyes closed and my mind focused. Something that I don't think I'm controlling.

Come to me, Krystal.

The voice is calling me, asking me to come. I guess I should listen since I am trying to contact a spirit and it seems as though I have. Only this isn't the spirit I want.

Opening my eyes slowly, I see that the clouds that had only begun coming in as I entered the cemetery now occupy the entire sky. The once sunny day is now gray and overcast. I had been walking toward the right side of the cemetery but instinct tells me the voice calling is coming from the left. So I take a step in that direction. Then another and another and then I see him.

As if he dropped right out of the sky, Ricky appears in

front of me. I jump back, screaming and holding a hand over my thumping heart.

"Jeez! You scared the hell out of me."

He laughs. *I doubt that, Krystal. You don't seem like you have a lot of hell in you to start with.*

I'm trying to calm my racing heart and shaking my head at him at the same time. "Whatever. Where've you been? I've been calling you."

He shakes his head. *You can't call me.*

"I did. I focused on you and I felt you answer," I say, all proud of myself for learning how to use a part of this power I had. "But then—" I start to say but he's still shaking his head, cutting me off.

I'm not there yet so I can't hear you calling me.

I blink, clearly confused. "Then how did you know I was here?"

You're my connection to the living world. I can always find you.

Okay, that makes sense. "I just can't call you?"

Not until I cross over. That's what Trina says.

"So, I could call Trina if I want?"

He shrugs. *I guess, but why would you want to call her?*

I think about the picture on my phone and wonder if I should call her to ask her why she was crazy enough to take a naked photo of herself. Or why she'd let somebody else take it. Either way, I don't know anybody who would send it to me.

Maybe Ricky knows.

How'd your visit with your shrink go?

He'd started walking and I just fell into step behind him, not real sure where we're going. Since we are in a cemetery, where the dead and probably undead hang out, anywhere we go isn't going to be very exciting.

"I don't need a shrink," I say, instantly defensive.

Nah, I don't think you do either. I just think you need

to snap out of this doom-and-gloom world you're deter-mined to walk in. But that can be done without your mother kickin' out a bunch of money to some crazy doctor.

"I agree," I say and surprise myself by really believing what he'd just said. Then I look at him, I mean really look at him, and realize something—he's transparent, like Trina and the crying girl at school, but he doesn't have that glow around him that they do. "So, where've you been? I thought you needed my help, but then you go and disappear. And why were you in the library spying on me and Franklin? That was so uncool. Plus, were you at the school today?"

He turns and then chuckles a bit. *Hold up, what's this, like fifty questions or something? First off, no, I wasn't at the school today. Did you see me there? And second, why are you hanging out with that clown Franklin? You wanna talk about "uncool," he's definitely it.*

"Franklin's a nice guy. Besides, it's none of your business who I hang out with." I guess that could go both ways, so my little jealous tiffs about him and Trina should be dismissed.

Like I said, he's a clown. Plus he doesn't even know how to step to you right.

"What's that supposed to mean?" I ask, then wave my hand to dismiss the question. "Never mind. Me and Franklin are none of your business."

He shrugs again. *Whatever you say. So what, you were looking for me?*

"Yeah, I guess I was."

And you thought you'd find me in the graveyard because I'm supposed to be dead.

"No, actually I remember reading that spirits frequent the cemetery. It's one of the few places they're totally comfortable. It made sense, so I came. And here you are."

Because I was looking for you.

"Really? Why?"

But before he can answer me my cell phone chirps. I have a text message. Digging it out of my purse, I press the button and gasp as the pictures immediately appear. It's not just one this time, but a couple of them, saved one after another. I'm using the little ball on my phone to scroll down and down and down until finally the last picture is revealed. One of Trina and another girl. It takes me a second or so—during which time Ricky is calling my name like he thinks I can't hear. I'm staring at the final picture not only because Trina is once again naked, lying on a bed with a really sleepy look on her face, but because of the girl. The one sprawled on the bed next to Trina, just as naked as Trina, her white skin a stark contrast to Trina's cocoa brown. Both of them have a similar glazed look in their eyes and slack look of the mouth, but that's where the similarities end. Not that I am searching for similarities, more like recognition I'd say. And damn if I don't find it.

The other girl in the picture with Trina is crying girl from the equipment room in school.

"Are you doing this?" I blurt out. "Did you take these pictures? Why are you sending them to me?" I take a step and thrust the phone toward Ricky. Obviously he can't take it into his hands but he does look down at the screen so I start to move the scroll ball upward so he can see all of them.

"I got one yesterday, too, and wondered who could be sending it. Is it you?"

He snaps, *Last I checked there were no cell phones in the afterlife.*

I start to respond with a similarly smart remark but the look on his face has me pausing. He looks mad. No, he looks pissed the hell off! His thick brows have kind of knotted across his forehead, his semi-thick lips are smoothed to a thin line and at his sides his fists are clenched, looking like something I wouldn't want to run across in a dark alley.

"Why would she take these pictures?" I ask quietly.

She didn't.

"So she posed for them?"

Ricky turns away.

"Did you know about them? I mean, she is your girlfriend."

She's not my girlfriend, he says quickly. Almost too quickly.

"She said she was."

She was, as in past tense. As in when we were both still walking, living, breathing and talking.

"As in when she disappeared?"

He pauses, looking at me like he is surprised that I know.

I guess this means you've decided to help me.

I hunch my shoulders. "I figure something has to be done."

You figure, or you and your friends figure?

"I guess you could say all three of us."

It's Ricky's turn to nod his head. I think he's trying to figure out what to say next, so I decide to help him along.

"What happened to Trina? Were you involved in her disappearance?"

He doesn't hesitate. *No. I wasn't involved. And I don't know what happened to her. And even at this point she's not tryin' to tell me.*

"I heard you were the last person to see her alive."

Some people have said that. I don't necessarily know how true that is.

"I don't understand. Now that you're both...um..."

He fills in the word for me. *Dead.*

"Yeah." I clear my throat. "Now that you're both dead, why doesn't she just go ahead and tell you what happened to her?"

Because I didn't ask her.

"You don't want to know?"

Listen, things between Trina and I were different and I don't want to go back through them again. After I was shot up she showed up trying to help me, trying to ease the passage she said. But it didn't work. So right now, she's not a big concern of mine.

"So what about these pictures? Why am I receiving them now if they aren't related to what happened to you?"

I don't know.

I hadn't even noticed that when we'd stopped walking we'd ended up right in front of Ricky's headstone. Looking down at his name, I bend and smooth away some of the leaves and debris that have fallen on it. Then suddenly, I'm really tired so I sit down. We stay quiet for a while. I would say we are enjoying the serenity but we're in the middle of the cemetery so I don't really know how much enjoyment you can get from sitting there. Still, I've made a spot right next to Ricky's stone. I'm sitting with my knees pulled up, my chin resting on my knees. Ricky finally leans against the stone, his back partially facing me.

"How come you hung out with those guys at school? They're troublemakers and you don't strike me as their type," I ask finally. After all, that was my reason for coming here. To call him and ask him more questions to help us figure out what is going on.

Because Twan hung out with them.

"Oh, come on, you're the oldest. Don't tell me you follow your kid brother's directions."

If it meant protecting him, then yeah, I guess I did.

"How were you going to protect him by joining them?"

I figured if I was on the inside I could watch out for him better. Make sure any stupid mistakes he might have made were covered up or kept him from getting hurt.

"Well, isn't getting mixed up with that type of group stupid mistake number one?"

He gives a little chuckle that doesn't quite seem like a laugh. *Yeah, I guess you could say that. But, you know, things aren't always what they seem, Krystal.*

"It seems like you and your brother both got hooked up in the wrong crowd. They're known for their violence and rudeness and I even heard they'd robbed some place before. Maybe you could explain what good could come from being mixed up with a bunch like that, because it doesn't seem all that appealing to me."

You're really naive, aren't you?

"What?" I'm quickly offended. "I'm trying to help you and you're calling me names."

I'm not calling you names, just making a statement. You're really naive. I kind of got that impression when I first saw you.

I turn so I can see him fully. "When did you first see me?"

It was during that snowstorm at the end of February. You came outside your house and just kept walking around, stomping in the snow like your footprints would somehow change the world.

It is mid-April so he's been watching me for about three months now, but I don't recall him saying anything to me. "Why didn't you say something sooner?"

I don't know. Waiting, I guess.

"Waiting to see if there was anybody else who could help you?"

He turns and looks directly at me. *No. Waiting to see when you'd be ready to hear what I had to say.*

His gaze is so intent on mine that those butterflies in my stomach start twirling around again. I notice I get this feeling a lot when I am around Ricky. At first it made me think I had a crush on him. Then I started talking to

Franklin. I like him, too, though the feeling is not quite the same.

"So what is it you have to say?"

Are you ready to hear it?

"Yeah."

I mean, are you really ready to listen? Not try to answer questions that you don't have answers to, but to really listen to my story, to what happened to me and to maybe do whatever you can in your power to help.

I nod my head once, but Ricky looks back like he doesn't believe me. And just as I'm about to nod my head again, my cell phone starts chirping. I'm almost afraid to answer it.

I don't want it to be Janet but since I'm almost an hour late coming home there's a good chance that's who it is on the other end.

I notice it says "unknown number." For a minute I think about the number that has been calling me on and off for the past couple of days that I don't know. Then I think about the text messages that show no number at all. Both make me hesitant.

It's on the third ring and I'm still debating because what if it's the person who's sending me the disgusting pictures? It's ringing and not vibrating and the noise is loud in the otherwise quiet cemetery. I decide to just go ahead and answer it.

"Hello?"

"Hey, Blue Bird. Glad I finally caught up with you."

My heart leaps with joy. I mean, really, it does. It starts to beat faster, a grin that I know probably looks childish and silly spreads across my face and my general feeling is happier at the sound of my daddy's voice.

"Hey, Daddy. I've been leaving you messages."

"I know and I've been meaning to call you back."

I pull the phone away from my ear and look at the screen

again, just to verify that this is not the number I am used to calling my father on.

"This is a different number. Are you calling from someone else's phone? Is your phone broken?" Which is a stupid question because if he was getting my voice mails then the phone had to be working.

"Nah, Blue Bird, my phone's fine. Actually, I've got a new phone," he says.

But all I can really focus on is that he's still calling me Blue Bird. He's been calling me that since I was four years old and they decided to paint my room. It took me only three seconds to point at the book full of paint colors and declare that blue was my favorite color in the whole wide world. I don't think I'll ever become too old to hear him call me that.

"So you've got two phones now. I don't understand."

"No. I'm going to cut the old phone off but I wanted to wait until I talked to you to make sure you had the new number first."

"Oh," I say like I understand even though I don't. Because really, how often do teenagers understand what their parents are saying?

"Listen, um, I've got something to talk to you about but I think it's best if I tell you in person."

"Really? So are you sending for me? When am I coming back to New York?"

"No, baby, I think I'm going to just make a quick trip up there so you and I can talk."

"Oh," I say, trying to mask my disappointment. "Well, when are you coming?"

"Probably this weekend since I'm moving next week."

"You're moving? Moving where?"

"That's part of what I want to talk to you about. It's a great opportunity. The comic strip might be heading to the movie screen. So I just need to tie up some loose ends here on the East Coast. I'll tell you all about that when I see you."

"Okay, Daddy," I say, my excited heartbeat now slowing to a confused stutter.

"So I'll be there this weekend. Be good, Blue Bird."

"I will," I promise but don't know how I can possibly be good when I'm talking to ghosts and staking out gangs. But I don't get a chance to say that—not that I would have anyway—because Daddy has already hung up.

For a few moments I just look down at the phone in my hand wondering what just happened. Is my daddy really moving? I thought that when I finally talked to him I'd have some answers or I'd feel differently about this situation with him and Janet. But now, after being on the phone with him for less than two minutes, I feel more confused than ever.

Your old man's coming to see you, huh? You feel better now?

My head snaps back as the sound of his voice reminds me that I'm not alone. "Feel better? What's that supposed to mean?"

Well, you've been acting all salty since I met you, pining away for your old man like he's your savior. So, is he coming to rescue you or not?

"Shut up! You don't know what you're talking about."

He just tilts his head, his hands are pushed in his pockets again, his legs spread apart in that stance he likes so much. He looks mean and careless and…like a gang member. *Now you think everything's going to be better?*

"As a matter of fact, I do," I say, holding my head up a little higher to convince him how confident I am in my words.

Ricky just shakes his head like he's sad or I'm sad or something like that. *Sometimes things aren't always what they seem, Krystal. Remember that and try to keep an open mind.*

"Are you talking about me or you?"

He looks at me with that intense stare. *I'm talking about both of us.*

twenty

The meeting that had been scheduled to take place in Sasha's pool house is mysteriously changed to Jake's house. I receive the call regarding the change of plans like ten minutes before Mouse pulls up in front of my house.

The moment I climb into the car I know Sasha is in a mood. Trying to be cordial, I ask if she is okay, only to receive a shrug and a mumbled, "Sure. I'm just fine."

She sits in the backseat of the little sports car with me in the front passenger side seat next to Mouse. We don't talk and that's fine. I have a lot on my mind and obviously so does she.

Jake's grandfather is already in bed when we get there, which is sort of a bummer because I like talking to him. And plus I have more questions about our power and this funny feeling I have that there is so much more to it than what we originally thought.

We head straight back to Jake's room where he has the computer on and some newspaper articles pulled up on the screen. He doesn't waste a moment, doesn't ask what's wrong with Sasha or why the meeting place changed, just jumps right in.

"Ricky's body was found in the early morning hours of

February 7. He was lying in the alley, not too far away from the school but closer to that run-down building that the hip-hoppers sometimes hang out in," he says.

"Why leave the body so close to your hangout spot?" I ask instantly. "I mean, wouldn't that automatically make you look guilty?"

Jake nods.

"They're all idiots anyway," Sasha adds, plopping down onto Jake's bed. She always does that, like it's her bed in her house. Only it isn't. I'm guessing that Jake's house is nothing compared to hers, considering her family is one of the richest in Lincoln.

We decide to ignore her and keep going. Jake reads from the computer, "'The body of an unidentified black male was found by two passersby around 3 a.m. The male had been shot three times in the torso, resulting in his death. At the time of printing, the Lincoln Police Department had no suspects or leads.'"

"So, who do you think killed him?" I ask.

"Don't know," Jake replies.

"I wonder if he killed his girlfriend, that Trina girl," Sasha says, lying flat on her back and twirling a long strand of hair around her finger.

"He didn't," I say quickly.

Sasha turns to look at me. "How do you know?"

"I asked him."

"You did? When?"

Jake's looking at me now, too, so I go ahead and answer. "When I tried to call to him earlier today. I went to the cemetery and was gonna, I don't know, summon his spirit."

"Wow." Sasha sits up on the bed, staring at me eagerly. "So did it work?"

I shrug. "Sort of."

"What does that mean?" Jake urges.

I inhale then sigh. "Ricky showed up but he said it wasn't

because he heard me calling, more like he was looking for me and found me."

"So your summoning didn't work?" Sasha says, sounding a little deflated.

"No. I think it did," I answer quietly. "I heard something, I mean, someone calling me. They wanted me to come and I was going to go but then Ricky showed up."

"You don't know who you heard?" Sasha asks.

I shake my head no.

"It's happening," Jake says.

I'm confused. "What's happening?"

"Our powers," he says solemnly. "They're manifesting."

Silence fills the room as each of us looks back at the other.

"How do you know? Was there something else in the journal?"

Jake nods and pulls out the old raggedy book I'd last seen earlier at lunch. He puts it on the desk and opens it, pulling out a very old piece of paper that he hands to me. I unfold it and read. It is the letter he'd IM'd us about, the one written by a Mary Burroughs and dated 1692. Apparently Mary was accused of being a witch and burned at the stake. As Jake starts to speak I pass the note to Sasha and listen.

"'January 1950. William is powerful. He can do things that nobody else can. Sometimes it's like he's possessed and others he seems perfectly normal. Ever since the first time I saw him move the furniture the power has grown. Now he's not only moving stuff that he looks at but just yesterday the old shelf in the garage was about to fall in on his pa when William just looked at it and it froze, just stopped falling right then and there. He moved Pa out of the way and with the blink of his eyes the shelf hit the floor in a loud crash. That night Pa said we should move and take William with us. People wouldn't understand what he was.

We didn't understand what he was. This morning when I got up William was gone.'"

"William Kramer, your great-uncle, was a Mystyx," Sasha says, rubbing her hand over the parchment paper she held. "And Mary Burroughs wasn't a witch at all. She was a Mystyx, too."

"I think so," Jake answers slowly.

Then there's a loud sound coming from outside, like something's being slammed against the side of the house. With one glance at each other we all get up and head to the back door and out into Jake's yard.

Well, it's not actually a yard, just a few feet of ground that used to have grass and is more like matted mud now. It's drizzling, a quiet mist falling peacefully. There's an old car parked on the side of the house; it doesn't look like it can even move, plus the tires are all flat, the silver rims touching the cement. There's a shed right across from the car but the whole front is missing. I remember seeing some wood propped against the house when we came in.

That's what Mateo Hunter and Pace Livingston are using to bang against the already dilapidated siding of Jake's house. I recognize them from school—Richies who are on the football team. Apparently Sasha recognizes them, too, because she keeps right on walking as me and Jake come to a halt outside. Right now she is reaching out, grabbing Pace by his beefy arm and halting his next swing at the house.

"What the hell are you doing?"

Pace turns, his unruly ash-blond curls falling slightly over his sweaty forehead. His eyes are green, like the ocean, but now look a little darker as he turns on Sasha.

"We're tired of him thinking he can do what he wants. He and his kind have no business hanging out with you!" Pace shouts.

"Yeah, we were riding by and we saw your car," Mateo, the taller of the two jocks, with skin the color of caramel candy and thick curly black hair, says. "He's gotta learn his place!"

"You're both idiots," Sasha yells, trying to take the strip of wood from Pace's hand. "Get out of here before I call the cops."

"No! You get outta here, Sasha. You don't belong here with them." Pace's words echo as his gaze lands swiftly on both me and Jake.

Beside me I can feel a change. It is still raining, that steady trickle of cool water hits my cheeks and bare arms. But in addition to that there is something else, like heat. Invisible waves of it simmer between me and Jake, and for a minute I am afraid. Then, as the heat circles around me and my neck also warms I know instinctively what it is.

The Power.

Just as mine is manifesting I have the sinking feeling that Jake's is, too.

Mateo continues to beat on the house until pieces of siding buckle and fall off, leaving a hole where insulation shows. The whole time he is whacking away at the house he is calling Jake names.

"Stupid Tracker! Dirty scavenger, trying to take our girls. Stick to your own kind! Stick with her!"

The insults go on and on until I feel like taking a piece of that wood and going upside Mateo's head myself. Instead Sasha throws herself on Mateo's back, grabbing his swinging arm to stop the next assault.

"Get her off me!" Mateo yells as Sasha's nails rake over his cheek.

Pace grabs her and Sasha yells. I step forward, ready to jump into the fight no matter what the cost, when Jake grabs my elbow, holding me back.

"My house. My battle," he says in a voice that does not sound like him at all.

"But Ja—" I start but he'd already pushed past me.

Standing right in front of me, Jake stops, fists clenched at his sides.

"Get off my property," he says and I swear I hear thunder roar behind it.

Pace, who had grabbed Sasha around the waist, turns to Jake and tosses Sasha to the ground. "Why don't you make us, Tracker!"

"Yeah," Mateo says, lifting his leg off the ground to break the wood over his knee. "Come and make us!"

This is so not good.

But Jake doesn't move.

I run around him to help Sasha, who keeps slipping in the mud as she tries to get up. It is when I finally get her up and can see Mateo and Pace heading for Jake that I see Jake's eyes.

Sasha must have seen it, too, because she holds my arm a little tighter.

He has a fierce look about him, Jake, that is. And even though the two jocks heading for him are three times the size of his slim form, he is holding his ground. Probably because he knows something those two beefy dumb jocks don't.

"I'm gonna beat you into the ground," Mateo says, continuing his approach to Jake.

"Then I'm gonna grind my foot in your neck, you dirty piece of shit!"

And before either of them can say another word the wood that was on the ground is suddenly in the air, swirling around until it is hitting both Mateo and Pace in the kneecaps. With girlie-sounding yelps, they both hit the ground. Apparently that isn't enough for Jake.

Near the shed are some garbage bags. Turning his gaze

in that direction, Jake lifts the bags, bringing them to hover over Mateo and Pace.

"Who's trash now?" Jake says a second before he turns the bags over so that the contents are emptying on the heads of the two jocks.

Sasha giggles and claps. Me, I don't know what to do. I am stunned by what Jake has just done. He'd actually moved those things with his mind. Then as I look down to the ground at Mateo and Pace rolling around in rotting fruit, beer cans, old coffee grinds and whatever else was in those bags, I feel a giggle of my own building. Soon both Sasha and I are laughing and the dumb trashy jocks are picking themselves up off the ground and running to their car.

"You're all crazy freaks!" Pace yells on his way.

They reach for the door handles and we hear a clicking sound.

"Get the keys, idiot," Mateo yells at Pace.

Digging into his muddy and dirty pockets, Pace fishes out his car keys, puts it in the lock and turns. But when he goes to pull the handle to get in, there is that clicking sound again.

"Jackass, what are you doing?"

Pace curses. "I unlocked it!"

He repeats the motion of unlocking the door again and then we hear the telltale clicking again and see Mateo kicking the passenger side door.

"I unlocked it, I swear!" Pace yells, looking down at his keys then banging on the side window of his car.

Behind us we hear a chuckle. Me and Sasha turn to see Jake smiling.

"You're doing that, aren't you?" Sasha asks him.

He only continues to smile, then reaches up a hand to rub the *M* on his arm.

It is warm, just as my neck is. Just as I'm sure Sasha's hip is.

Jake is right, our powers are manifesting. That could be a good thing. Or more likely, I think but wisely keep to myself, really bad.

twenty-one

Ur so cute. Wish I had a pic so I could c u all the time. Want 2 kiss u. Touch u. Hold u. Number1

Um, now I'm officially scared. Who is this? And why's he stalking me? I should call the police or at the very least tell Janet and Gerald.

At the top of my phone screen there's no number listed, just the screen name "number1" like it's been programmed into my phone. That's new. It wasn't on the messages with the pictures. But something tells me they're both coming from the same person.

Too creepy, I think as I drop the phone back into my purse and close my locker. Turning around, I bump right into Franklin. I thought I was in the hallway alone so coming face-to-face with him almost has my heart leaping out of my chest.

"Whoa, it's just me, Krystal," he says quickly, reaching out to grab my wrist because I am about to start swinging. "I didn't mean to scare you."

I let out the breath that had clogged my lungs and lean back against the locker. "Don't sneak up on me like that."

"I wasn't sneaking. Just waiting for you to finish so I could walk you to the bus stop."

I try to smile. Franklin's so nice. And I think he's trying to be like a boyfriend or something. Unfortunately, between supernatural powers, spirits needing help, naked pictures of students on my cell phone and a tense home life, I'm just too whacked out to really appreciate his efforts.

"I'm sorry," I say, hoping that's good enough. I really don't want him to ask me what has me so jumpy.

"You okay, Krys? Is there something I can do to help?"

I shake my head quickly. "No. I'm fine. Thanks. And I'm not going to the bus stop today, got a meeting."

"Oh? I didn't know you were on the yearbook committee," he says.

"I'm not."

"Well, that's who's meeting this afternoon, unless you're trying out for the basketball team."

In the time we've been chatting, Franklin hasn't moved an inch. He's still directly in front of me, so close that our fronts are touching. This makes me feel warm and I wonder if I should move. But just as I think I should, he takes a step closer.

I clear my throat. "Ah, no. I'm not doing either of those. Just meeting with a few friends."

"Can I come?"

He's touching a hand to my face now.

"Um, no. It's kind of private."

He nods his head. "I really like you, Krystal."

Ohmigod. Ohmigod. Ohmigod. Does this mean he's about to kiss me again? Ever since first meeting Ricky I've been obsessed with getting my first kiss over with. Knowing it will never be with Ricky, Franklin is the next best candidate. Besides, I like him, too.

I open my mouth to say that but Franklin's quick and his lips are on mine before a sound can come out. Now, since my mouth is slightly open, the first kiss seems a little awkward. But then Franklin does it again. This time his lips touch mine (closed) lightly and when he pulls back he looks right into my eyes.

"Will you be my girl?"

Ohmigod. Ohmigod. *Stop it!* I yell at myself for acting like a ninny.

"Sure," I say, and it sounds all breathy like one of those women on television.

Franklin smiles. "Good."

The next time he kisses me I close my eyes and lean into him. His arms come around my waist, pulling me even closer to him. I'm all tingly inside and just know this has to be like heaven.

"Oh, please, get a room."

The nasal-sounding voice interrupts us and Franklin and I quickly pull apart. But it's only Alyssa.

"Why don't you try getting a life," I snap. This girl is seriously getting on my nerves.

"Yeah, just as soon as you accept your place and stop trying to be something you're not."

"Come on, Alyssa, be nice," Franklin says.

She looks at him then frowns. "Poor Franklin, I thought you had potential since your father's, like, semifamous being on the news and all. But hanging out with her is so déclassé."

And she is so full of it! I move from the locker and make a move toward her but Franklin pulls me back.

"See what I mean? She's ready to fight like some street person. You can do so much better," she says and starts to walk away.

I reach out an arm like I'm going to grab some of that fake hair hanging down her back but Franklin just chuckles and pulls me away.

"She's not worth it," he says, draping an arm over my shoulder.

"She's a bitch," is my retort.

He shrugs. "You might be right. So anyway, you're going home after your meeting?"

"Yep," I say because I know that Janet and Gerald want to have another family dinner. And I don't really know why but I'm thinking it might not be all that bad since we're staying at home this time.

"So I'll call you later?"

I smile. "You can."

"I will," he says, then kisses me once more and leaves the building.

I'm, like, floating down the hallway as I go to meet up with Jake and Sasha. But as I'm walking, voices in one of the classrooms stop me.

Standing on tiptoe, I look through the lone window in the classroom door and see Mr. Lyle. He's in there with a bunch of kids, mostly girls, and they're all sitting around this long table talking. That's not what catches my eye, though. On a corkboard right above the table where they're sitting are more pictures. One of them looks vaguely familiar. I'm trying to figure out where I recognize the face from when it dawns on me that I'm already late meeting Jake and Sasha.

So I move away and start walking down the hall. Only a few steps in and I hear a door opening behind me.

"Ah, Krystal. Interested in joining the yearbook committee?"

I turn and see Mr. Lyle staring at me. I didn't think he'd seen me peeking in but I guess he had.

"Ah, no. I was looking for another meeting," I say quickly.

"But we could use another person on the committee.

Another pair of eyes," he says and then looks at me weird, like he can see through me or at least through my clothes.

Ewwww, perv!

"No, thanks," I say and quickly make my way down the hall and around the first corner even though it takes me past the stairwell that I was supposed to meet Jake and Sasha in.

Counting to fifty, I wait, hoping I've given him enough time, then I circle back and head toward the stairs. That's when I see something on the floor. It's like its rolling, coming straight toward me.

A sense of dread bubbles in my stomach and even though I want to run down those steps I can't. I'm stuck right here staring down at the same eerie black smoke that I saw at the library.

How did it get into the school and what the hell is it?

It's getting closer and I want to investigate. I want to know what it is and if it's connected to this new power I have. I think it is. Don't know why, maybe everything creepy going on now is related to the Power. I don't know but I'm ready to find out.

I take one step then I'm yanked back so hard I think my arm is being pulled out of its socket.

"Where've you been? We've been waiting and waiting," Jake says. "I was getting worried."

Once I'm inside the stairwell I pull my arm from him. "Okay, okay. I'm right here, you don't have to rip my arm off."

Then he kind of shrinks back against the wall, giving me the saddest, most pitiful look I've ever seen. I'm instantly sorry for yelling at him. Then again, he should be sorry for yanking on me.

"Look, I apologize. You just scared me."

"I scared you? Why, what happened? Did you see another spirit? Is somebody following you?"

"No," I answer then look at him for a minute. "Why would someone be following me?"

"I don't know. I was just saying."

No, I think, *he isn't really saying anything at all.* But I have a feeling he wants to.

"As a matter of fact, I think somebody, or something, might be following me."

Jake lifts up from the wall, looking at me seriously. "What? Tell me what it is."

I tilt my head. "I think you're gonna tell me."

"Krystal," he says like he's tired.

"Okay, remember I told you in front of the library there were these birds and then this black smoke was like smothering me?"

"Yeah."

"Well, I saw the smoke again. As a matter of fact, this is the third time I've seen it."

"Where else?"

"In my dream," I say slowly. "The first time I went to the cemetery and found Ricky's grave was in my dream. I was running and suddenly the fog was there. It stopped me. I couldn't run anymore."

Jake is quiet.

"What is it, Jake?"

He doesn't answer right away.

"Jake!"

"I don't know!" he yells back. "I just don't know. I read the whole journal and it doesn't say what 'it' is." He pauses. "Just that 'it's' coming. It's coming for us."

twenty-two

sasha appears right in between us the second he says that.

"What's coming for us?"

I turn to her, shocked to see her even though I know she has that teleportation power. "Where were you?"

She looks over her shoulder at me. "Since you were taking so long I teleported myself down to the room to take a listen to what the hip-hoppers were saying."

"And?" I ask just as she turns her attention back to Jake.

She waves a hand over her shoulder, not turning back to look at me. "Nothing much. As it turns out, their big meeting was about what they are wearing to the dance. Can you believe that? Like they're girls or something."

"So you didn't learn anything about who might have killed Ricky?" Jake asks.

"No. But Antoine did mention that his aunt had found some e-mails on Ricky's computer. Something about him keeping his mouth shut or paying the price. She said the e-mails weren't from any of the kids at school so that clears the hip-hoppers of Ricky's murder."

I take this information in, thinking about the weird text

and IM messages I've been getting lately. Although none of them insinuated that I know something.

"Now that I've delivered my information, why don't you two tell me what you were talking about before I arrived?"

Jake looks at me and I look back at him and shrug. Finally he says, "Come on, let's talk and walk."

Jake thinks there's something coming.

Franklin said his father thinks a big storm is coming, too.

Me, I think these powers are deeper than any of us ever thought. Sure, we have these matching marks and we can do some pretty cool things, but I have a feeling there is more to it.

In the past people were accused of witchcraft and killed. Some of them were probably just like us. It stands to reason that there might still be people in the world who would want us gone because of our differences. But Jake isn't sure that's what we should be afraid of.

"Throughout the rest of the journal, Eleanor talks about this 'darkness.' Sometimes she just says 'it.' Whatever, it's bad. William was never seen or heard from again. Or at least until the end of the journal, a couple weeks before Eleanor died in 1978. I asked my grandfather but he said he never saw his brother again after that."

"Does your grandfather have powers, Jake?" Sasha asks as we walk through the parking lot to her car.

Jake shakes his head. "Says he wished he'd get them someday but they never came." Jake takes a deep breath then sighs. "He said that my mother was really afraid of getting pregnant. She'd heard stories about the Power and the storms here in Lincoln. She came from down south, he said."

I've never heard Jake talk about his mother before and I'm not really sure how to handle it. Then again, if it's going to help us figure out what is going on, I have to say something. "But I don't think it's just in Lincoln. I mean, Mary Burroughs was in Massachusetts. All those storms in 1932, the year William was born, were in different places. No matter where she was when a storm hit, if she got pregnant her child would have the Power."

"Yeah, I think so, too," I agree.

Sasha looks thoughtful. "What does your dad say?"

"I didn't ask him. He doesn't like to talk about it. Pop Pop says that's why my mom left, the first time she saw me use the Power. She was afraid of what would come next so she just left."

I nod, understanding all of a sudden now why Jake's home life is the way it is. "And your dad blames you for that. He blames you for chasing your mother away. That's why he doesn't spend time with you."

Jake looks away and I can't help but feel sorry for him. So while usually he's the one touching me, I put my hand on his shoulder and kind of rub a little.

"He's wrong, Jake. It's not your fault at all."

Sasha chimes in, "She's right. It's not your fault. We were born like this. Blaming us for what is, is just stupid."

We're all standing there thinking on what we've just discovered when overhead loud screeching erupts. I know what's above us before I even look up because I've seen them before.

Three black crows are swooping down, heading straight for us. I lift my arms up over my head and Sasha does the same. Jake stands still and stares at them, like he did that day in his yard with the jocks, but nothing happens. The screeching grows louder and I feel one of the birds nip the skin of my arm.

"Get in the car!" Jakes yells but I can't move.

The bird is nipping at me like he's starving. There's one over Sasha, too, and I see Jake swinging at the one near him. Then Sasha's gone. She disappears.

In the next minute I hear the engine of her car start and the passenger side door swings open. Jake makes his way over to me and grabs me by the waist, pulling me to the car while we both keep trying to fight the birds off. Jake shoves me inside then dives in behind me. Sasha pulls off with his legs still hanging out. He rolls over on the seat and pulls the door closed.

For a couple of miles the birds fly right above the car. Then, as suddenly as they appeared, they're gone. And when me and Jake turn back to look out the window I see it.

The black fog, rolling along the ground behind the car.

"You see it, don't you?" I whisper but don't know why. "Please, tell me you see it, too?"

Beside me Jake nods. "Yeah, I see it."

The minute my head hits the pillow I fall asleep. Today's been eventful plus I didn't get much sleep last night what with my little visitor showing up. Praying I don't have another visitor tonight, I let my breathing fall into a level pattern and try to rest.

Obviously that is not meant to be, or maybe I do sleep for a while at least.

All I know is that at some point cold fingers moving along my skin wake me up. I think maybe it's just chills since my sheet has fallen off me but when I reach for it, it's not there. I move my feet thinking I'll find it but it's gone. Must have fallen on the floor.

So I lean over, switch on the lamp and let out a scream that could surely wake the dead.

Oh, my bad, the dead are already awake and they're standing in my room!

When the screaming is so loud I think my head is going to explode I thrust my fist inside my mouth to stifle the sound. I'm beginning to think my screaming must be a part of these dreams or else Gerald or Janet should have come running by now. I'm still scared out of my mind as I'm staring at at least ten corpses lined up around my room like bodyguards.

They all look old with raggedy clothes hanging from their bones. Bits and pieces are missing from their faces—that's probably why I'm still shaking with fear. They're ugly and scary and...they have that same glow around them that Trina does.

I remember wondering why she had that glow and Ricky didn't. The woman on the beach and the girl in the school had glowed, too. I think now it's because they've already crossed over, like these other dead folk have.

With my heart still hammering, I finally get up enough nerve to pull my fist from my mouth. Of course I'm drooling like I did that time my mouth was numb from having a tooth pulled. My hand is now wet and just a little sore from my teeth baring down on it. I wipe it against my shorts and try to speak again.

I'm trying to gain control. I'm the medium, not them. They have no power without me. (I read that online, too.)

"Who...what...I mean...why are you here?"

The one at the end, the taller one with what looks like remnants of a suit barely holding on to his bony frame, turns to me and acts like he's going to walk closer.

I start moving backward until I hit the wall and then I'm like a spider, practically crawling upward to get away from the ghost.

We're here because you can help us.

I'm already shaking my head no. "I can't help you. You're dead." Like I need to remind them of that.

But you can hear us, we have messages.

"I'm not a messenger," I say even though I know I am, sort of. I wonder if I inadvertently called them here, like in my sleep or something. Our powers are stronger now that we've all linked up and they will continue to grow. I have no way of knowing what I can do at this point.

We know you can hear us. There aren't many who can.

"I can't help you," I say, my voice sounding deceptively stronger.

She lies! another one shrieks. This one is close to my closet with long, dirty—I guess it used to be hair—hanging down her back. *She won't help us! Let's take her.*

What? Take me where?

Okay, here goes that scream again. And I pray this time that someone living hears me!

I'm still screaming when they all start moving toward me. I start to pick up stuff, whatever is close to me, throwing it at them. When I finally yank my lamp out of the socket and hurl it at them, not only does the entire room go dark but a loud crashing echoes in the darkness.

twenty-three

"calm down, Krystal. Take deep breaths," Gerald is saying, his warm breath brushing over my face, his thick hands squeezing my arms. He's shaking me, not hard, but like he's trying to get me to snap out of it.

I feel like a rag doll, my body limp in his arms. I try to speak but my voice is a dull rasp and hurts like all get-out. The pain brings tears to my eyes even before I see Janet silently crying beside me.

Gerald sighs. "Calm down and tell us what happened. You broke the damn window."

He's upset and Janet's crying. I'm trying to scream—again—but the sound is buried somewhere deep in my chest. My eyes can't hold out anymore so tears rush down my cheeks. When Gerald finally lets me go I crumple to the floor. It takes Janet a few seconds before she kneels down beside me and rubs a hand over my head.

I instantly pull up my legs and let my forehead rest on my knees. Just a few minutes ago my room was full of spirits, but they seemed different than the ones I'd seen up till now. Angrier, more dangerous. I threw the lamp in an effort to keep them away from me. I guess the lamp broke the window.

The sequence of events really doesn't matter now. Gerald is pissed. I see him crossing the room and punching numbers into his cell phone. I don't know who he's calling but I'm almost positive my stay here, in this house with him and Janet, is now officially over.

"What happened?"

Dr. Whack Quack is sitting across from me with his notepad and pen. He's watching me like I'm on a fifty-inch flat screen. Then again, that's how they all watch me here in the hospital.

I've been here for almost two days—they can only keep me for observation for forty-eight hours. Then they have to prove that I'm crazy enough to admit me. Janet won't say that I'm crazy. I heard Whack Quack trying to get her to admit it when they were standing in my room and thought I was asleep. Gerald hasn't really said much, which is surprising.

But Janet keeps crying, keeps insisting this is all her fault and that I just need my dad.

She is kind of right.

Only I think I need her *and* my dad.

"I had a bad dream," I say simply.

Whack Quack nods. "So you threw the lamp out the window?"

"Have you ever had a bad dream?" I toss back at him.

"I have," he answers.

"And has it ever scared you so bad you felt you had to protect yourself?"

"Yes."

"Then you already know what happened to me."

"But I've never thrown a lamp out the window."

I roll my eyes. "Well, hooray for you."

He taps his pencil against his chin, still watching me. "I wonder if this is more like a cry for attention."

I don't say anything because he didn't ask me a question. I'm only going to answer his questions so I can get out of here.

"Do you want to get your mother's attention?"

I shake my head and answer honestly, "I want my mother to listen to me."

"What are you trying to tell her?"

"That I'm unhappy. That I want things to go back the way they were."

"And what if that's not possible? Are you prepared for that answer? What are you going to do if she says things have to stay the way they are?"

I shrug because I never thought of what her answer might actually be. For so long I've just wanted to say that I'm not happy. I don't really know how I think she's going to fix that.

"Do you think your mother is happy?"

"I don't know. Sometimes it seems like it, but the other day she was crying."

"Do you know why she was crying?"

"I don't." That's a lie. Janet was crying because I yelled at her.

"How did you feel when you saw she was crying?"

Like an idiot. "Sad," I say instead.

"Did you want to help her? Do anything to keep her from crying?"

"Kind of."

I shift in the chair; it's uncomfortable now. This office isn't like Whack Quack's other office. This one is all white, with no comfortable chairs and no books. No clocks. I don't like this one.

"What can I do to help you, Krystal?"

"Let me go home." And when I say that, I'm surprised that I'm thinking of the house I live in with Gerald and Janet.

"Do you think you'll throw anything else out the window?"

"I can't predict what my dreams will be." Or who will try to haunt me in those dreams next. More than just those spirits scared me, it was the knowledge that there's something else, something dark, lurking, waiting for me and Jake and Sasha.

"I want your mother to join us in our next discussion. I think there are some things you two need to talk about."

I look away from him because I don't know if Janet will talk to me and I don't know if I'll be able to say anything to her. It feels like I want too much and scares me to think I may never get any of it.

"Blue Bird," Daddy says, his arms wide open as I make my way back into the hospital room.

I'm so happy to see him I run right into his arms. Now I know that everything is going to be okay. It doesn't matter that Whack Quack made me feel bad today, that what he's saying makes me sound like I'm a spoiled brat and need to get myself together—kind of what Ricky said, too. But I don't want to hear it from either of them.

"Hi, Daddy," I cry, hugging him tight.

He hugs me tight, too, lifting me off the floor and spinning me around. I love the feel of his arms around me. It makes me feel safe. He smells like cologne, a great manly scent that I relate only to him. And when he finally releases me, he kisses my forehead and then my cheeks.

"You okay?" he whispers, his hands cupping my cheeks, lifting my head up so I can stare right into his eyes. Eyes just like mine.

I nod my head, too emotional at the moment to speak.

"You scared about ten years off my life," he says, breathing heavily and laying my head on his chest for another hug.

"Sorry," I mumble.

Then he moves to the bed. He sits and I sit beside him.

"So tell me what's going on? Why are you destroying furniture and breaking windows all of a sudden?"

I shrug but then Daddy looks at me funny, like he's not accepting that answer.

"I had a nightmare," I say because it's true. Whether the grown-ups want to believe me or not. I'm not about to say it was dead people asking me for help because I know I'll never get out of here if I do.

"And that made you break the window?"

"Somebody was attacking me. I thought I had to defend myself. I'm not crazy, Daddy."

He chuckles. "I know you're not crazy. But I also know you have a temper. So were you mad with somebody when you did this? Gerald maybe?"

Daddy knew me well. I did have a temper, or at least I used to. Since moving here to Lincoln I didn't have much of anything. "He gets on my nerves," I say instantly.

Daddy laughs. "I figured."

"But that's not why I threw the lamp. I told you I was scared and I was trying to stop whoever was attacking me in the dream. That's all."

"Your mother says you haven't been eating."

"Not real hungry, I guess."

"Self-imposed hunger strike?"

I kind of smile. "No."

"Yeah."

"Can I just go back to New York with you? Because that'll make me feel better. I won't be angry. I'll eat. I'll sleep and not dream."

Then Daddy's whole face changes. He's not smiling anymore. His eyebrows kind of straighten out and so does his posture. His arms fall from my shoulder and he puts his hands in his lap.

"That's kind of why I'm here, Krystal."

Uh-oh, he didn't call me Blue Bird.

"Some producers bought the comic strip. They're talking about making it into a movie. So, ah, I'm moving to L.A."

I take a minute to digest what he said. "Oh. Well, that's good news," I say, trying to sound upbeat. "So I can go to L.A. with you?" I don't know if I'll like living in California. But anything has got to be better than Lincoln.

"No. You have to stay with your mother."

How did I know he was going to say that?

"Why? I know a lot of kids who choose which parent they want to go with. I'm choosing you."

"I know, but our situation is different. Your mother needs you and you need her."

"I need my father. And why did you get a new phone?"

He looks like I caught him off guard. He turns to me and then says, "Amanda and I both have new phones now. We're on the same account."

I pause, pull my head back and stare at him. I know I'm looking at him like he's crazy but that's because I'm trying to figure out what he just said. "Amanda?"

I only know one Amanda. I don't know how many Daddy may have known.

He lets out a deep breath. I mean, his cheeks puff up and I actually watch as the air blows out.

"Yes. Amanda. She's going to L.A. with me."

Okay, I'm old enough to know about the needs of men and women. I've witnessed my mother leave my father and marry Gerald—the creep. So it stands to reason that if there is no possible way my parents are getting back together—which seems perfectly clear to me at this point— that Daddy would get a girlfriend or a wife, too. I don't have to like it, Janet has already proven that point. But at least this time I'm going to ask the questions I want.

"So this Amanda person can go to L.A. with you but I can't? Does she live in New York? Why don't you just leave her there?" My voice sounds snippy, with a lot of attitude and just a pinch of spoiled brattiness. I don't like it but I can't help it right now.

"Amanda and I are engaged," Daddy says finally. He's not looking at me now but then he turns and stares directly at me. "She's going to have a baby."

If he had smacked me I wouldn't have been more shocked. If the sky had opened up and whisked me away in a dark, blustery tornado I couldn't have felt more winded and confused. "A baby? Your baby."

"Yes."

And just as I'm about to ask my next question, there's a soft knock on the door. And in she comes—without being invited, I might add.

The only Amanda I know.

She is tall and skinny—well, except for the stomach that looked like she was carrying quintuplets. Her hair is long and brunette, shining like a mink coat as it hangs past her shoulders. Her eyes are still light, gray I think, her lips pouty but spreading into a smile as she looks at me.

Amanda Spinelli, my old babysitter. The one who used to sit in my room and read to me while Janet and Calvin were at work. She was young. Younger than Janet and much younger than Calvin.

My stomach starts to hurt, that hot pain that I thought was only reserved for Janet.

"How pregnant are you?" I blurt out.

Her smile falters only a bit before she says, "I'm almost due."

Almost due means nine months, right? We left Daddy and New York nine months ago. Janet got a quick divorce but I didn't think of why. I assumed she just wanted to hurry up and be rid of Daddy because she said he needed to grow up. Not because he was moving on...with Amanda.

"You cheated on my mother with my babysitter?" The question is bitter, accusatory, and so is my glare at him.

He stands up from the bed, Calvin Jefferson Bentley, the man I love so dearly, the one I looked up to and waited to rescue me.

"That's grown folks' business and something I'm not going to discuss with you."

"Doesn't matter. I'm not stupid," I say, folding my arms across my chest. "So you and Amanda and your new baby are moving to L.A. to start a new life. A life without your first child?"

"It's not like that, Krystal. You'll always be my daughter. You'll always have a place in my heart."

I nod my head. "Like an old shoe or a first car? I get it."

"Don't be smart," he says, a frown etching across his brow.

"You can always come and visit," Amanda offers.

I chuckle. "Yeah. Right." Like that little family scene is ever going to take place.

twenty-four

silent tears fall, sliding down my cheeks to land on the pillow. They've created a wet spot but I don't care. I just don't move my face so the cool yucky feeling doesn't bother me that much. Besides, the heavy pain in my chest is much worse.

Are you disappointed with your father?

I remember Dr. Whack Quack asking me.

Hell, yeah! I feel like yelling, but my voice is gone.

Are you disappointed with yourself?

Yep, I feel like an idiot. I believed my mother was wrong, that she'd left my father without even giving him a chance. Actually, I figured she wanted to make me suffer, too, except when she started crying.

Inhaling deeply, I try to keep my lip from shivering. I feel like a fool. And what makes it worse is that I still haven't said anything to my mother. Gerald was with her when she came into the room. Calvin and Amanda had still been there but I ignored them. Even when Calvin tried to hug me and tell me he'd call me later tonight. I just sort of let him do all the hugging.

I noticed that my mother didn't look at Calvin or Amanda. Gerald looked pissed, like he wanted to leap across the room and pound on Calvin. They'd suggested I stay in the hospital one more night, just so the staff could watch me as I slept. I wanted to go home, but then I was too tired to argue so I didn't. I just curled up in the bed and lay there.

"I love you, Krystal," my mother whispered in my ear as her hands brushed my hair back. "I'll be here early in the morning to get you. Okay?"

I only nodded because my throat felt clogged and I knew words weren't coming out. Then I felt another hand on my back.

"Get some rest. You'll come home tomorrow and we'll put this all behind us."

That was Gerald. The calm tone to his voice surprised me. I thought I should probably say something in return or at least look at him but I was just so tired of all that's been going on that I couldn't. I just closed my eyes and wished for a few minutes of peace.

I'm at the school, that much I know. There are no lights on so I'm kind of stumbling through the halls. Then I hear the crying and walk faster, trying to get to the girl I know is sitting on the floor in the equipment room.

Only this time when I get there she's not there. For a minute I just stare at the spot where I saw her last. It's empty yet I still hear the crying.

"Shut up!"

I hear the man's voice and I turn toward it. His back is facing me, his dark clothes giving him the appearance of a big lump of black.

Her crying gets louder and I take a step in their direction. "Stop it! Stop it! Why are you doing this to me?" She's sobbing louder and her voice sounds familiar.

He pulls back an arm and punches her. The sound is sickening and I gasp.

"I told you to keep your mouth shut! Never, never tell anyone what we do together. I told you!"

"But I didn't tell. I didn't, I swear!"

"Yes, you did, because you're just like her. Just like that other tramp! Can't keep your trap shut long enough for me to make my money! Well, now you're gonna wish you had."

He hits her again and I run to them to stop this madness. He drops her to the floor and I see her face. I cover my mouth to hold in the scream. The moment he turns to me, my sight is filled with black smoke, choking me until I roll over coughing.

Click.
Click.
Click.

The flash from the camera is blinding me. Why isn't he using a digital instead of this ancient 35mm? That's my first question.

Then I look to the bed to see what he's taking pictures of. It's a girl, her teenage body naked but for a feathery wrap.

"Take it off," he orders gruffly.

Her arms move slowly, clumsily.

"Hurry up, I don't have all night."

She's trying but she can't seem to get her movements together. Then she finally gets the wrap off and falls back on the bed. I don't look at her body but at her face and feel a tightness in my chest.

Camy.

I spin around, trying to figure out where I am but all I see are photos—on the wall, on the floor, on the tables. Pictures and pictures of girls, young girls, naked girls. I feel sick but that doesn't stop me from bending down and picking up a couple of the pictures.

One is of Trina.

One is of Camy.

And the other…is of crying girl from school. But her face isn't pale or bloody. It's pretty, her red hair like flames. She's not crying this time but she's not smiling either. She's just lying there while a man touches her.

Then I know I'm going to vomit. I roll over, off the side of the bed and let the wretched images in my mind go.

twenty-five

Driving home the next day my mother is still quiet. I think she'll say something to me, ask me if my father had told me about his plans. But she doesn't. I wonder why she just didn't tell me about Amanda and the baby in the first place because now I realize that she knew all along. So even though I feel stupid for blaming her all this time, I'm still angry with her for keeping the truth from me.

I'm so confused now as I fall tiredly into my bed. I don't know who to trust or who to believe. Adults just do what they want, say what they feel is necessary and forget about you the rest of the time.

Everything is not always what it seems.

I hear the voice and truly am too tired to even lift my head to see him. He's been gone for the couple of days I was in the hospital. He hadn't once tried to contact me. That fact alone hurt my feelings but I guess I should get used to it. Ricky's dead; he can't be with me forever.

At least Sasha and Jake had called my cell phone, sent me text messages to make sure I was okay. And Franklin, I'd received texts and voice messages from him several times a day. Now, him, I could be with.

I'd told Sasha and Jake about the spirits trying to kidnap

me because I knew they'd understand. Sasha seemed really freaked out. Jake said he'd do some research because there had to be a way I could control their comings and goings. Franklin just thought I had the flu. That was for the best. I just appreciated the fact that now I had friends.

I didn't grow up with either one of my parents.

He keeps talking and I keep crying, the tears now a mixture of how I feel about my parents and how I thought I felt about Ricky.

My parents left me and Twan. I was seven and he was six. They just said they decided they didn't want kids and gave us to my aunt Pearl. She tried to give us everything they didn't. But me and Twan, we kinda figured we could raise ourselves after a while. Did some things we probably shouldn't have. But by the time I thought about that it was too late.

I sniffle and try to covertly use the pillowcase to wipe my nose before turning to face him. Mentally I remind myself to take that gross pillowcase off before I go to sleep tonight.

"I don't mean any harm, Ricky," I say, shifting in the bed so that my back is now to the wall and I'm sitting cross-legged in the middle of the mattress. "But I'm really not in the mood right now. I've got so much other stuff going on in my head, I just can't focus on you and your problems." And being this close to him is confusing me.

He shrugs his shoulders. *We're not that different, you know. Most kids have the same problems, just different circumstances.*

"Oh, did your father sleep with your babysitter, too?" I try for flippant but it comes out as a whine.

I don't know. He wasn't there, remember?

Right, he did say that. "So, I don't understand."

Like I said, different circumstances. You wanted your parents to be together, to be a happy family like the Cosbys.

Me and Twan, we wanted the same thing. Your dad slept with another chick, your mom got pissed and rolled out, taking you with her. Both our parents just split, no explanation, no looking back. Same problems, different circumstances.

He's absolutely right. I can admit that now without resenting him for it. "I see what you're saying."

But you've got to move on, Krystal. You ain't never goin' be able to make your parents, or any adults for that matter, do what you want them to do or what you think they should do. You gotta learn to roll with the punches.

I had actually sort of come to that conclusion myself. "It just feels like I've been sucker punched in the gut."

He smiles this time and lifts his leg up, resting his arm over his knee. He's in his favorite spot—the window seat—sitting there like it was built just for him. I don't know why but I like seeing him there.

Yeah, that's how disappointment feels. Been there, done that.

"I get the feeling you've been a lot of places and done a lot of things."

Oh, yeah. He nods. *And not all of them have been good.*

"Tell me what happened the night you were shot," I say, surprising both him and myself. I'd never asked him that before and the fact that I'm doing it now, when my own life is in shambles, is strange. Still, I want to know. I feel like I need to know to make that final connection.

The crew was meeting in that old warehouse by the school. I hadn't been around much because me and Trina were going through some things. We'd been beefing a lot in the weeks just before that. And then she was just gone. I was trippin' 'cause I didn't know where she was but I thought she might be in trouble.

"What kind of trouble?" I ask, wondering if he knew who had been taking those pictures of her. I know I'd asked him before and he said he didn't but now it sort of sounded like he knew something.

He looks at me, shakes his head then looks away. *She was taking those pictures. The one you got on your phone.*

I can't help it, I'm curious. "And you wanted her to stop?"

Hell, yeah, I wanted her to stop! I told her she was better than that, better than some porn star wannabe making money for people she didn't even know.

"And she didn't listen?"

Nah. Said she had a good thing going and that if I wasn't with her I was against her. He chuckles. *I don't know where she got that crap from. I just wanted her to be safe.*

"And you didn't think this was safe?"

No. Letting some perv take naked photos of you is not smart and eventually it wouldn't be safe.

"Some other girls around town filed complaints about some guy sending them IMs and text messages about sex. I read in the paper the other day that they also found photos in the girls' rooms. Photos that someone had taken of them."

Yeah? Nasty. What kind of man takes pictures of young girls?

I shrug. "The girls say they can't remember what the guy looked like. Said he might have given them some kind of date rape drug or something."

See, that's exactly what I think happened to Trina.

And he was trying to stop her, to protect her. I could see Ricky doing that. He has that protective nature about him, that's why he hung with the crew and looked out for his brother.

"So after you didn't see Trina anymore you just went back to hanging with your crew?"

Ricky sighed. *Yeah, I was headed to the spot when I heard something behind me, sounded like keys dropping on the ground, so I didn't think anything of it. A few minutes later something hit me in my chest and stung like hell. I stumbled a bit then looked down and saw the blood on my shirt. I touched it to make sure it was real and that's when I was shot again and again. Last thing I remember was hittin' the ground.*

"And you didn't see who it was that shot you?"

Nah.

"But you're sure it wasn't one of your crew?" The more I think about it, I am sure it wasn't either.

I'm positive. Why would they shoot me? I was one of them. Plus those guys aren't as bad as they'd like people to think. None of them have a gun or probably the guts to use one.

I smile at that, remembering that Sasha had said their big meeting was about what they were wearing to the spring dance. That didn't sound too big and bad to me.

"Do you think Trina knows how she died?"

Yeah, she knows.

"And she won't tell you?"

Why should she? There's nothing I can do about it.

"What do you think I can do about the person who killed you?"

You can expose whoever it is as a murderer and clear Twan and the crew's name. I don't want people to keep giving them a bad rep for something they didn't and could never do.

For the first time since I'd met him I really get what he is saying, what he is trying to do. This is so not about him, or simply his crossing over. Ricky has unfinished business, he has to clear the hip-hoppers' name and he won't move forward until he does that.

As for me, I'm not going to move on until I find out who did this to him and who that man is in my vision, the one who is planning to hurt another girl in Lincoln.

twenty-six

BEING a teenager should not be this emotional.

This should be the easiest, most enjoyable time in my life. Instead it's the most confusing, most unrewarding. Stepping out of the shower, I'm blasted with cold air. Shivering is a given as I try to dry off in record time. Slipping on my robe, I stand in front of the mirror while tying the belt around my waist.

I look old. Older than my fifteen years. And I feel about fifty.

My comb and brush are right where they normally are, which means that not only did my mother pack my bag to go to the hospital, but she unpacked it when I returned earlier today. I don't know how I feel about that just yet. So I try to focus on the pressing matter of my tangled flyaway hair that makes me look more like a wild jungle woman than a young girl. I probably should have washed it but I really didn't feel up to the full magnitude of that task. Wash, condition, blow-dry, style. My stomach's growling and I'm really tired so my plan is to finish in the bathroom, make a quick run to the kitchen then back upstairs in my room. I do not want to see or talk to anybody else until tomorrow. Today has just been too damn stressful. (Yeah, it is definitely worth the profanity—no matter how old I really am.)

By the time I'm finished in the bathroom my head is hurting—I probably should have sucked it up and did the whole wash-and-style thing. Instead I manage to untangle and probably pull out a good portion of my hair and pull it back into a semineat ponytail. My face still looks a little drained but it doesn't matter, I'm not going anywhere.

Back in my room I slip on some pajamas (the full set, long pants and T-shirt). I'm still a little chilly although I think it's pretty warm outside. Maybe Gerald had my mother turn up the air-conditioning. I see the window I'd broken has already been fixed and the room that was a mess when I left is cleaned. I didn't notice that while Ricky was here.

I'm wondering if I should log on to ChicTeen and IM Sasha and Jake with the new developments or if calling them would make more sense. My train of thought must have been translated to my only two friends in the world because there is a soft knock at the door followed by my mother's voice saying, "Krystal, honey, you've got company."

Luckily I am dressed and as decent as could be considering I'm in my bedroom and it's, like, after seven at night. My feet are bare as I walk across the floor just as she's opening the door and entering my room with Jake and Sasha right behind her.

I'm happy to see them since I have a lot to tell them, starting with the new info I got from Ricky and ending with the scary visions I am now having.

I look at my mother, who looks almost as bad as I do, and I don't really know how I feel about seeing her. Except that she's carrying a pizza box. My stomach growls and I know that I am, for once, grateful for her always trying to get me to eat.

"Hi, Krystal," Sasha says first, coming from around my mother to grab me into a hug.

It's weird, this relationship between me and Sasha. One minute we're snapping at each other and the next, well, she's hugging me.

"We were worried about you," she says as she's pulling back.

"I'm okay," I finally manage to say and smile because she's smiling at me.

"Girl, your hair is a mess and we've got to do something about that scar."

She pokes at my cheek and my hand absently goes there to trace the bumpy reminder of another one of my spiritual visitors, the one I think was trying to tell me who she really was. "Yeah, I guess you're right."

"I'd already ordered you a pizza," my mother says, holding up the box. "It's your favorite, extra cheese and pepperoni."

And then I do something that I know she's not expecting—sort of like Sasha just did with me. I smile at her and say, "Thanks. I was getting hungry."

And my mother smiles back, a real smile, one that makes her eyes sort of light up and makes me feel really happy.

"Well, I'll just leave this here. I brought up some plates, too, and Jake was kind enough to grab the soda and cups."

As she speaks Jake holds up the soda and cups, giving me a wry smile as he does.

I chuckle and shake my head.

"So I'll leave you guys alone for a while," she says, then makes her way over to me. "But I don't want you up too late. You need to get some rest."

I nod my head as she's talking. She's reaching out a hand and I know that means she's going to touch me. She hasn't done that in a long time. Her fingers graze my cheek, the scarred one, and her forehead wrinkles a bit. "I've got something for that. We'll put it on before you go to bed. Is that okay?"

She's the mother, why's she asking me? I don't know the answer but I decide to take Dr. Whack Quack's advice and answer her questions. Hopefully if I do that, she'll answer some of mine when I decide to ask them again. "Sure."

She's smiling again as she moves closer and drops a kiss on my forehead. She smells really sweet, like cookies and flowers. I've missed that smell.

The minute it's just us in the room Sasha opens the box of pizza that my mother left on my desk. She picks up a slice and drops it on a plate then plops down—that's right, you guessed it—on my bed like it's hers.

"So what happened? I mean with the ghosts and all. Your messages didn't really say."

The sound of Jake releasing the top from the two-liter soda echoes in the room. "Please answer her," he says with his back turned to us as he starts pouring the soda into the cups. "She's been rambling about this for the past two days. We even tried to get into the hospital to see you but they wouldn't let us."

Hmm, they'd come to the hospital…to see me?

I move to the table and pick up two slices of pizza and a cup of soda. Then I make my way to the bed to sit on the opposite side from Sasha. I pick the pizza up and take a bite, not thinking of it coming back up or getting stuck in my throat. This time I focus on the taste, the tangy sauce, the smooth kind of bitter cheese, the spicy pepperoni. I feel my stomach churning in hunger and know that I'm going to clear this plate to make it stop.

"At first I thought I raised the dead," I say between bites two and three.

"Wow!" Jake pauses, his pizza just inches away from his mouth. "You did? How?"

"I didn't really know since I was asleep. I was sleeping

and then I woke up and they were here, a bunch of them right in my room. They were asking me to help them and when I said no, one of them got angry and threatened to take me with them. That's when I freaked and started throwing stuff at them, telling them to leave me alone."

"And that's how you broke the window?" Jake asks.

"How'd you know I broke the window?"

"I came by your house that morning. Pop Pop had gotten up at breakfast rambling on and on about the Power and a storm coming. So when neither of you answered your phones I decided to come by. But when I got here nobody was home. I saw the plastic over the window."

"And when he finally caught up to me at my house we figured something might have happened because of Ricky so we came back to your house and waited until your dad came home. He told us you were in the hospital."

She's talking about Gerald and I want to say he's not my dad. But for right now I guess he's the closest thing to it.

"I've been thinking about our powers manifesting and I really don't want dead people showing up whenever expecting me to stop whatever I'm doing to help them."

"Then you have to control it, Krystal. You're the only one who can. I think as your power continues to grow you'll figure out a way to deal with it. We have to be responsible about these powers."

"We're teenagers, Jake. How responsible do you think we'll be?" Sasha quips.

"As responsible as it'll take. We can't have others finding out about us, asking questions, making a big deal out of it. We don't know enough about this power ourselves to explain. So, Krystal, you've got to come up with a way to deal with the dead and what they want from you."

I'm chewing a particularly chewy piece of crust when I say, "Okay, well, what do you think of this for manifesting? I think I had a vision."

"A vision?" Sasha asks.

"Yeah. I mean, I went to sleep at the hospital and then I was in the school and it didn't feel like a dream, it felt like I was really there. And the pictures were real, just like the ones on my phone."

Jake and Sasha both stare at me like I'm the newest star in that vampire movie, totally hanging on my every word.

"So what do you think?"

"Wow!" Sasha says.

"Wait a minute, you didn't tell us about any pictures," Jake says.

No, I didn't. I'd kept a lot from them but I know the time for full disclosure is now. So I grab my cell phone and find the message with the pictures. Then I go to my desk drawer and pull out the first newspaper article I'd seen on the pervert sexting and IMing young girls in Lincoln.

"I think it's all connected," I say, plopping back down on the edge of my bed.

"All connected to what? Trina's death?" Sasha says, scrolling through the pictures on the phone. "Hey, I know this girl."

"Where, which one?" I ask and am not surprised when she pulls up the picture with Trina and the red-haired girl, the one I know from the equipment room and from my vision.

"Her name's Charlotte—"

"—Ethersby." I finish for her. "She's the one who scratched my face." They both look at me funny. "She was here in my room the day after I saw her at school in the equipment room crying. She wrote her name on my mirror but I didn't know who she was until you just said it."

It's quiet for a few seconds then Sasha says, "Whoa, this is big."

Jake nods. "This is huge. You're saying that somebody's running a teenage porn ring in Lincoln."

I nod. "Yeah, I think so."

"And that he killed Trina."

I shrug. "Maybe."

Sasha puts the cell phone down. "But who killed Ricky?"

"He doesn't know, but I think that might be connected to Trina and those pictures. Ricky said he'd tried to warn her, to get her to stop."

"So what if she finally listened," Sasha is saying. "Tried to back out and the person making the money from the pictures got mad, killed her and then killed Ricky, too, for good measure."

That would explain the message on the blackboard: *MONEY. PICTURES. LIES. KILL.*

"Sounds like a Lifetime movie," Jake says.

Both Sasha and I look at him. "You watch Lifetime movies?"

"No," he says, a crimson blush on his cheeks. "Pop Pop does and sometimes I just work on my laptop in the same room so I can keep an eye on him."

"Uh-huh," Sasha says, nodding. "I'll just bet."

We all laugh and for the first time in my life I feel like I belong. Like these friends actually belong to me.

It's a good feeling.

One that tries really hard to mask the fear of the unknown. The unknown we know is coming for us and the unknown we need to uncover to set Ricky free.

twenty-seven

Franklin came over today. Only I don't want to stay in the house because it is nice outside. Tomorrow is Monday and I'll be heading back to school after my little hiatus. Me, Jake and Sasha had talked until late last night, so late my mother had to come in and tell them it was time to leave.

The consensus was we needed to do something. If I was having visions, we figured they were either of the past or the future, probably both. So Camy might be next to die. And while she wasn't on my favorite persons list, I didn't exactly want to start seeing her all transparent and glowing in the afterlife either.

Most of the morning I'd spent at my computer searching random things like visions and weather, witches and supernatural beings. I'd tried to search black fog but hadn't gotten anything tangible to go on. I didn't find out much about those vicious birds either. So by the time my mother came up and told me I had company, I was happy for the reprieve.

Seeing Franklin in his fresh-pressed khaki pants and crisp white shirt was shocking but refreshing. Yesterday I'd spent time with Ricky and my feelings for him had been so conflicting. In the end I knew that they could lead nowhere but to heartache. But with Franklin...there were possibilities.

So we're walking in the park, right along the path where Ricky and I had walked before. Franklin's holding my hand, a fact that I think is cute and makes me feel really special. He's talking about something but I'm not really listening. Well, I am kind of, to his voice, but not really his words.

He's already gone through that squeaky puberty change and there's this smooth timbre to his voice that I like.

"So, you're going to the dance with me, right?" he's saying as we get closer to the little pond.

Today is a really nice spring day, kind of breezy, bright with sunshine. Perfect to be walking in the park with your boyfriend.

"Huh? Oh, the dance. Um, I wasn't going to go," I say finally.

"But you have to, you have to be my date. You know, since you're my girl."

He stops walking and turns so that he's standing in front of me now. His hands slip around my waist and I put mine on his shoulders. Here's something else I like, being close to Franklin.

"I hadn't thought of it that way. You hadn't already asked somebody?" I say, thinking of Alyssa. She acted like she wanted Franklin for herself and she's pretty so I could see him wanting to go out with her. I guess.

"No. Who else would I ask?"

"Alyssa, maybe."

He laughs. "Please. I don't have the patience to deal with that girl. She's way too high maintenance for me."

I smile. "And I'm not?" I'm feeling really good now knowing that he really doesn't like Alyssa in that way.

"No," he says, suddenly real serious. "You're not high maintenance. But you're special."

At first I feel alarmed. "Why do you say that?"

Franklin lifts a hand and pushes my hair back behind my ear. I've worn it out with only a headband today and the breeze is having fun with it. This, his soft touch, calms my nerves a bit. "I knew you were the first day I saw you. Special, I mean. I just had this feeling."

"Oh," I say because I don't know what else to say.

"You're special to me, Krystal. I don't want to go with anyone else."

I nod my head. "Okay, then I'll go."

"You will?" He's all smiles now.

"Yeah, I will. But you'd better not let me see you dancing with Alyssa."

He just shakes his head and I feel his hands tightening around my waist, pulling me closer. "I'm going to dance with you all night and then when I go home I'm going to dream of you. And when I wake up, I'll think of you."

"Dancing with me will be enough," I say, kind of embarrassed by his words.

Then he leans down, because he's a couple inches taller than me, and kisses me. I hug him closer, welcoming the next kiss and the next.

And for this moment in time everything in my life is perfect.

Then I hear the squawking above and the perfection is replaced with dread.

Home life hasn't been too difficult, all things considered. I still haven't talked to Calvin and I guess he's already in L.A. with his new family. It's so crazy how all these months I've been waiting on him to call, to come and get me, to rescue me from my mother and her new husband. He never had any intention of rescuing anybody. Come to think of it, since he's so into moving these days, maybe he instigated ours.

I don't know and there's really too much going on in my life right now for me to try to figure out. A few weeks ago I thought my parents getting back together would be the answer to everything. Now, I'm starting to think differently.

"Hi, Krys, how was school?"

Janet appears from the kitchen as soon as I walk through the door and drop my book bag in the hallway. I don't run straight to my room now. For some reason, lunch just isn't enough and I usually want a snack by the time I walk from the bus stop. My mom still can't cook so dinner is always an experiment, except when she orders out or I go to Jake's with Sasha—which we've been doing a lot.

"School was okay," I say, refusing to think of creepy Mr. Lyle and the quiz he said I'd failed. All this supernatural stuff is killing my study habits.

"The dance is tomorrow and I noticed you didn't charge anything on my card when you went out the other night."

She is referring to the night Sasha picked me up to go to Jake's. Sasha's excuse was that we were going shopping for a dress to wear to the dance. Janet then handed me her credit card.

Humph, busted.

"Ah, no. I didn't really see anything I liked."

She just smiles. "That's because you're so hesitant about going."

I shrug and go ahead into the kitchen. "I guess you're right."

"So why don't you want to go, really?"

I'm in the refrigerator, grabbing a handful of cherries and a bottled water. It appears that she wants to talk and since I'm not doing anything else I figure why not. So I sit at the table and she joins me. It seems strange but comfortable now that we're in the small kitchen, sitting at a table with only four chairs instead of being in that huge dining room with twelve chairs and a mile-long table.

"Well, at first it was because I didn't really know anybody here."

"And now you do. Sasha and Jake seem really nice."

"Jake is. The jury's still out on Sasha."

She laughs. I like the sound and realize how much I've missed hearing her laugh and laughing with her. I smile and let a chuckle escape.

"You wouldn't believe how moody she is. One minute she's all nice and friendly and the next she makes you want to slap her silly."

"Oh, I hope you haven't hit that girl."

"Not yet, but she's asking for it, I'll tell you that much. She gets too smart sometimes and I have to put her in her place. I keep tryin' to tell her just because I'm quiet doesn't mean I'm a wimp."

"No. I don't think you are," she says thoughtfully. "And what about Franklin?"

I knew she was going to ask me this. "Franklin's really nice."

"And really cute," she adds.

I can't help but smile. "Yeah, that, too."

"I think he really likes you."

I shrug. "I guess so. I mean, I like him, too, but I had to make sure he didn't like this nasty girl at school named Alyssa."

"Oh?"

"Yeah, I was just like, 'Are you going to be dancing with her at the dance or with me?'"

She raises a brow. "And what did he say?"

"He said he didn't like Alyssa and that he was only going to dance with me. Which is a good thing because I don't play that two-timing stuff." I feel bad the minute I say that but she doesn't look like she minds.

She looks down at her hands, rubs a finger over her new wedding ring. "You're right, Krystal, you're no wimp."

We are quiet for a minute and then I say, "And you're not a coward."

Her smile slips and she adjusts herself in the chair. She looks like she's about to be all serious and that's not what I want. I just want to kind of clear the air between us, you know, get some things off my chest so I don't explode.

"I'm just saying that I shouldn't have called you that when I didn't know the real story."

"And now you do? Know the real story, I mean."

"I know that he's got Amanda pregnant and she looks like she's ready to bust so I figure he must have been messin' with her when he was with you."

She doesn't say anything right away and I take that as a yes. Her smile is completely gone now, her lips are pressed tightly together and she runs her fingers through her long black hair.

"I think maybe I should have been a little more up front with you, Krystal. About why we were leaving New York. I just didn't know how. You're my little girl, telling you things like this seem wrong."

"I'm not a little girl anymore, Mama. And keeping important stuff from me doesn't help."

She sighs. "You were so mad at me."

"Because I didn't understand."

"Well," she says, taking a deep breath then letting it out, "I guess we were both wrong."

"Yeah, I guess so." And that's that. We've apologized and we'll move on.

"Do you want to know why I left him?"

I hurry up and shake my head no. Then I sigh. "Yes."

She nods. "I left him because he cheated on me with Amanda and Lord only knows how many other women.

See, this wasn't Calvin's first outing but it was the last one I planned to settle for."

"You shouldn't have stayed for the other ones," I say, feeling an unsavory bitterness bubbling inside for the man I thought was my father.

"I know that now. But I had to give it a chance, for you."

"You stayed with a cheater for me?"

"I didn't have a father growing up. It was just me and my mom and then she died and my grandmother came here to take care of me. I wanted my baby to have a real family."

"An honest mother would have been enough," I say and really mean it. If I had to live with a lying, cheating father then I'd rather not have one at all. If he could lie and cheat with everyone else, he'd do the same with me and I was better off without him.

"I'm glad you finally left him."

She sighs. "I'm glad I did, too."

Then, since we are talking about her and Calvin, I figure this is the best time to ask about my conception.

"You met him in New York, right, while you were in college?"

She blinks a little, probably at the shift in conversation. "Ah, yes, we did. I was in my second year when I met him at an art gallery. I was there with a couple of friends just goofing off and he was there staring at the paintings like they were the greatest thing since electricity. You get that from him, you know, your love of drawing."

I did know that and up until a few days ago had been very proud of that fact. Still, it didn't stop me from picking up my charcoals and pad and drawing again. It had been too long since I'd allowed myself that freedom. I wasn't going to let my disappointment in Calvin stop me again. "I know," I answer simply. "Did you ever bring him back here? I mean, did you, like, live in Lincoln for a while before me?" She shakes her head no and I think of our theory that the Power is also born outside of Lincoln. "He never met Grams before she died?"

"Oh, yeah, he did. But we weren't here that long. We came up for the Thanksgiving weekend. Your great-grandmother loved to cook a big meal, but after I left she didn't have anybody to eat it." She laughs and I can tell the memory of Grams is still painful for her.

"We only planned to stay until that Friday after Thanksgiving because your father had a strip due on Monday and he wanted to work on it at home. Calvin could only work in the loft with his supplies, in his surroundings, he'd say. But when we woke up Friday morning I remember Grams saying we couldn't get out. There was a storm watch and they'd closed the roads off and were fixing levies by the water."

"Wow, you were here for a blizzard?" I ask, already knowing it wasn't a snowstorm that time.

"No. It was rain. I mean a hurricane. I know that's virtually unheard-of for this high up the eastern shore and in November, but it was definitely a hurricane. A huge one that knocked out the power and a lot of the buildings around us. Some houses just floated out into the Atlantic afterward. It was tragic."

Okay, so is now the time when I say, "Did you and Calvin get busy in Grams's house during the storm?" Probably not, no matter how much progress I thought my mom and I were making. I'm just not convinced that's going to go over too well.

Instead I say, "That must have been some Thanksgiving memory."

And just like I'd hoped, she gets this faraway look in her eyes then looks back at me and smiles. "It was a memory that I took back to New York with me."

"Really? How?" This clueless act is getting on my nerves but I'm so close to her saying what I want to hear.

"Because that's when you were conceived."

Bingo!

I giggle to make it seem like that is the last thing I expect her to say. "Cool."

"So, you see, it made sense for us to come back to Lincoln, to start over."

I nod my head even though a few months ago I wouldn't have agreed with her. "This town's starting to grow on me." Then as an afterthought I add, "At first I didn't like Gerald much."

"I could tell."

"I didn't think he liked me either."

"He didn't like that I didn't tell him about you as soon as we met. And then when he saw you he didn't like how you'd instantly taken Calvin's side. Until I told him that was my fault for not telling you what had happened between us. Anyway, I wouldn't stay with him if he didn't like you, Krystal."

As if I'm not already feeling like a big jerk for being mad at my mother, now Gerald seems like he might be okay, too. Jeez, just how wrong could one person be? "He seems moody like Sasha, probably just a teenage thing. Maybe he'll get over it," I say and laugh to lighten the mood.

"Maybe."

Then she does something I don't expect. She stands and comes around the table to stand beside me. "I know you said you're not a little girl anymore, but I'd be so happy if I could just get a hug."

For a minute I think of saying no or coming up with some excuse but then I look at her, really look at her. Her eyes don't look as tired as they have been for the past few months. She's not wringing her hands like she's going to rip them off at any second. She looks calmer, dare I say happier.

I wonder if I'm the reason for that or at least part of the reason. So I stand up and wrap my arms around her waist.

It's funny, at fifteen years old I'd like to think I'm past forehead kisses, packed lunches and hugs that hold you tighter than leather. But I'm not.

I love the feel of her arms around me, of my head resting against her chest, of the rhythmic patter of her heart against my ear. I love her scent that reminds me of when I was a baby and rested my head in this very spot. But what I love most of all is what she says to me next and how it fills me up completely.

"It'll always be you and me, Krys. No matter what."

That's better than I love you, better than I miss you or I'm sorry. Why? Because it says that no matter how dumb and spoiled I act or how misunderstood she is, that we'll be together.

I like that. Very much.

twenty-eight

"**You're** beautiful," my mom says as she looks at me through the mirror.

She's standing behind me as I'm surveying myself and trying to keep from looking up at her. If I look at her, I'll see that she's happy, happier than she's been in a long time. I feel bad and sad at the same time, and then I'll feel happy that we're together. And then I'll want to cry like she's doing. So I don't look at her.

Instead I run my hand over my stomach, acting like I'm smoothing down my dress. It's so pretty, I have to admit. I would never have picked it out for myself but I'm glad she did. It's royal blue with a collar like a button-down shirt except it has sparkly white rhinestones on it. There's a belt with a rhinestone clasp at my side and then the dress flares out like one of those ladies on *Dancing with the Stars*. It's so cool because even though it has a collar there are no sleeves. On my left wrist is a sapphire tennis bracelet that my mom had given me for my fourteenth birthday and around my neck, resting coolly against my *M*, is the matching necklace. On the other arm she says Franklin should put my corsage.

"Thanks," I say finally and turn around to face her.

"I'm so happy you're going," she says and pulls me to her for a hug.

"Ah, okay, Mom. I'm happy I'm going, too," I mumble, blinking furiously because this mascara she put on me has my lids sticking together.

"No," she says and pulls away, cupping my cheeks in her hands. "I'm happy that we're talking again and that you're eating and we're both happy. I'm just—"

"Happy?" I interrupt.

She starts to laugh and so do I.

"For the record, I feel the same way."

Then we hear the doorbell and I know Franklin has arrived. For a second I feel like Cinderella, then as I move down the steps I feel something else.

Anticipation? No, dread. Of what might happen next.

Cold out 2nite. Temp has dropped

That's the text I get from Jake while riding in the car with Franklin to the dance. I text back:

ino gt a jacket

We're sitting in the backseat and Franklin reaches for my hand. It's after eight so it's dark outside, dark in the back of Franklin's father's car. My cell is in my other hand since I took it out of the small purse my mom bought to go with the dress when it vibrated.

im freezing

Sasha texts me. And I'm about to text her back something trivial about wearing a coat over that strapless minidress she insisted on buying but then I think about what they're both saying and instead type:

think ths is the storm???

I text this to both Jake and Sasha, suddenly worrying that the temperature drop from yesterday's sixty-two degrees and this afternoon's sixty-four to this evening's forty-seven means more than just put a jacket on.

maybe

Jake responds.

definitely

Sasha texts.
I'm inclined to side with Sasha.
So I stare out the window, watching the dark sky and the quiet streets of Lincoln as we pass by, wondering what's in store for this little town and how it will affect me.

Franklin's dad, his name is Mr. Walter, he seems really cool. He'd been talking and joking since we first got into the car. Then it dawns on me that since he is being so friendly I can probably get some info about these storms and how we could possibly get power from them. So I learn that all storms carry energy, sometimes heat energy or cold energy and even electrical energy. He thinks our storms are spiked by all three of these elements, that there's an unusually high level of energy in each of our storms.

The Power, just like Pop Pop said. Only as a scientist, Mr. Walter thinks of it in a textbook way. Actually, he talks like he believes these freak storms and the energy spikes might be widespread. He actually sounds excited by that prospect.

He's confirmed my thoughts—our thoughts—that these

storms are happening all over. Which means there are more out there like us, more with this Power.

Franklin lifts an arm and puts it around me. I snuggle a little closer to him because I'm suddenly chilled by the thought of more Mystyx. And as my head rests on his shoulder I'm touched with another thought.

The logic of light and dark, cold and hot, up and down— if there is a good power, which I am certain the Mystyx have, then there has to be a bad.

As Franklin and I enter the dance, Beyoncé's "Single Ladies" is blasting through the gymnasium. There're already a bunch of kids in the center of the floor dancing. Over the top of their heads are strands of crepe paper in all different colors. On the walls are more crepe paper and balloons and other weird-looking paper objects. It looks like the party store exploded in here when just yesterday I was in here standing in my squad line going through daily gym class roll call.

Franklin's holding my hand. Has been since I climbed in the back of the car. I wasn't sure he'd keep doing that once we got here, but he is. Butterflies are dancing in my stomach, for Franklin this time, because he's touching me, because we're a couple. I'm smiling and people might think it's because they're speaking to us but it's not, it's because for once in a very long time I'm happy.

The DJ changes songs and I spot Sasha. She's on the dance floor with Twan. I think they look cool together. Sasha with her exotic coloring, designer dress and flawless makeup and Twan with his black baggy jeans, white button-down shirt and black boots. He wasn't wearing a hat today and his hair was neatly cut around his cocoa-brown face. He looks like Ricky a little. His face is a little fuller and he doesn't have the dimple, but he's still cute.

I get this funny feeling about the two of them, like there's something there but they're both fighting it. Well, maybe not Twan since he's grinding up on Sasha like he's ready for whatever. But definitely Sasha, she has a lot of resistance where Twan is concerned. I just hope it's not solely because of who he hangs with and how he dresses.

I see she's looking a little uncomfortable by the way Twan's moving on her so I start walking in their direction.

"You wanna dance already?" Franklin asks, sounding kind of surprised.

"Not really," I say quickly. "I was just going over to speak to Sasha."

"Well, she looks busy so we might as well join in."

He pulls me to the center of the dance floor and I wave as Sasha looks up and sees me. She smiles and takes that opportunity to back up a little from Twan. I kind of shrug, hoping she gets my message that it's okay to keep dancing with him. Then she nods her head like she's approving of Franklin. Again, this bond between us is weird but it's growing on me.

The song shifts from something hip-hop to "You Belong With Me" by Taylor Swift. It's a cool song and I'm actually feeling like the lyrics are directed right at me and Franklin. He said he thought I was special and that he cared about me, well, I felt the same way about him. I know that now, am absolutely certain about it. So I guess he does kinda belong to me.

The thing about happiness is it really depends on what's happening at the moment.

Here I am on the dance floor with a really cute boy, my boyfriend. I have another friend dancing with her guy— whether or not she wants to admit that's what he is. And we're at a school dance, being teenagers, enjoying ourselves.

And then I see it.

Or I should say her.

Camy and Alyssa enter the gym looking like they just stepped off *Project Runway.* Their dresses are definitely designer and definitely expensive. Their hair is fabulous and their dates—I hate to admit it, are hot! They don't even look like they go to Settlemans, which is strange because this is the only high school in town.

But it's like all of that slipped away in the background as I zero in on Camy. Why? At first I don't know but then it hits me. She's wearing a hot pink dress, asymmetrical, touching one knee on one side and riding along her thigh on the other. It's held up by spaghetti straps made of rhinestones. Her shoes are silver, strappy and studded with more stones. Her blond hair's all curly, falling around her creamy shoulders and...it's exactly what she was wearing in my vision.

Immediately my heart starts to race. Tonight's the night. I know it. From the funny feeling I had when I was leaving the house to the sudden drop in the temperature and now this. Whatever is coming after us is here and whoever is going to kill Camy is going to do it tonight.

twenty-nine

scanning the room, I look for Sasha and Jake. We need to talk, to figure out what we're going to do.

I find Jake. He's leaning against the wall looking like this is the last place he wants to be. His faded pants and hoodie have been traded for black slacks that fit him a lot better and another T-shirt, but this one is a shinier black material and he has it tucked into the slacks. He looks cool, hip, for the first time.

Obviously someone else thinks so, as a short, skinny girl grabs his hand and pulls him to the dance floor. He looks like he's anything but comfortable, but the girl looks persistent. She has a pretty smile and a really round face. She's Asian, I can tell instantly by the slanted eyes and coal-black hair. She's cute and doesn't waste any time plastering her tight little body against Jake's. His cheeks turn red and I feel sorry for him because he's totally embarrassed. Then again I feel a little happy for him because I hate to see him so quiet-looking all the time.

Like he realizes I am looking at him, he looks over at me. I smile and lift a hand to wave. He lifts his hand slowly, sort of moves his fingers back at me, but doesn't smile. He looks totally out of his element. The warning stirs in me again and I want to use this as a reason to rescue him. Then I think, maybe I'm meant to handle this alone. The part about Camy, I mean. It was my vision after all.

"Hey, what's up?" Sasha is tapping me on my shoulder and I jump because I didn't realize she is behind me.

"Ah, I'm, ah, thirsty," I say quickly and glance at Franklin.

He nods. "I'll get you something. Sasha, you want a drink, too?"

Understanding me completely, Sasha says, "Sure. Thanks a lot, Franklin."

The minute he's gone she grabs my arm. "Something's going on. I can feel it."

"Yeah. Me, too. I don't know what, though."

"We should get Jake," she says.

I look in that direction again. "He seems, ah, busy."

Sasha follows my gaze. "Who's that?"

I shrug. "I don't know, exchange student, maybe?" I had never seen the Asian girl around the school before but that didn't mean anything since I hadn't been in town that long.

"Okay, well, what should we do?"

"Camy's here and she's wearing the dress I saw in my vision."

"Oh, no," Sasha gasps. "We've got to warn her."

"How? Walk up to her and say, 'Hey, Camy, saw you getting bashed in the head, just wanted to give you a heads-up'?"

"No, that'll never work," Sasha says like she really thinks I'm serious. "Maybe if I go and keep her occupied for the rest of the night."

"But what if it happens after the dance?"

It's Sasha's turn to shrug. "I don't know. Wait! She's leaving."

I see it, too. Camy's heading toward the door, alone.

"Let's follow her," Sasha says.

I agree but then I hear my cell phone. Sasha is already moving to go with Camy as I pull out the phone and look at it.

U look gr8 2nite. Cn we meet?

It was number1 again and this time I knew exactly what I had to do.

Sure. Where?

This is beyond crazy and yet I know it's what must be done. Number1 has to be the perv getting young girls to pose naked, texting all this sex talk and then killing them. And if he is, then he killed Charlotte and probably Trina. And, I think what I've been suspecting the past day or so, Ricky.

So with my heart hammering in my chest, my palms sweating, my legs shaking as I take the stairs toward the hallway where he asked me to meet him, I begin to think about my power. It's not a very physical power and I don't know how it'll help me in this instance but it's moving through my veins, filling me with a confidence I've never possessed before.

I know where I'm going, past the gym and around the corner to where the locker rooms and equipment room are. He wants me to meet him in the equipment room, where I first saw Charlotte. I wonder if that's where he killed her.

He is clever. He will try to trick you.

I hear the female voice and while it startles me I don't flinch, just keep moving.

"I'm not afraid of him," I say to the air or the spirit who's with me and realize that I mean it.

That's what I thought.

A different voice this time, one I recognize. I look around for Trina but she isn't there, at least not in her spiritual body.

I should have said something sooner, I know. But I couldn't. I was afraid.

"Ricky said he told you to stop," I say just as I approach the door to the equipment room. "Why didn't you?"

I don't know. Guess I don't love Ricky as much as you do.

Whooooaaa, who said I loved Ricky? Like him a whole lot maybe, appreciate that he really listened to me and gave me the kind of advice I needed to hear, but no, I'm almost positive I don't love him.

He's going to do it again.

This is Charlotte speaking now. My hand is on the doorknob as I pause because maybe there's something else she wants to tell me.

You must stop him.

I nod. "Okay."

That's all I can say. I know he's dangerous, I know he's a pervert and that he's killing young girls. What I don't know is how I'm going to stop him.

Taking a deep breath, I open the door and step inside. I don't even get a chance to look around before I'm grabbed around the waist and slammed face-first against the wall. He's big, his body pressed up against mine, and he's strong.

"Finally," he says, breathing hard in my ear.

The voice sounds familiar…get him to say more, keep him talking. If I can buy some time, Sasha's going to get Jake and they're going to come looking for me.

"You didn't ask me to meet you in the other messages," I say, struggling to stay calm.

"No, but I wanted to."

His hands are moving over me, touching the dress my mother had bought, making it feel dirty now instead of pretty. I want to vomit, truly, honestly just puke at the thought of this grown man—because yeah, he sounds old—touching me like this.

My teeth are sinking into my bottom lip to keep from screaming. "You wanted a picture. Is that what you do, take pictures?"

"Oh, yeah. I've got lots of pictures."

He leans in closer and touches his tongue to my neck. I shiver. He chuckles and I know who he is.

Struggling, I try to get out of his grip but he holds me tight. I want to run, I want to get away from him because of who he is. What he can do to me is more terrifying than anything I've ever thought. But then I remember Charlotte and Trina and even Camy and I go slack against the wall.

"If you want to take a picture, then come on." I know I'm baiting him but I don't know what else to do, how else to handle this. The room is really cold. I can hear the wind blowing outside; it's pounding against the windows.

Again I think of the Power. Mine. Sasha's. Jake's. The unknown darkness that we know is coming for us.

It's strange but again I feel confident and strong. I take a deep breath.

"Trina looked good in her pictures. But Ricky didn't like them, did he?"

"What?"

"He wanted her to stop letting you photograph her, right?"

His fingers are tightening around my waist and it hurts but his upper body is pressing against me, holding me still.

"Trina was stupid, she had a big mouth. You wouldn't tell, would you, Krystal? You didn't tell about the messages I sent you or the pictures. You're a good girl."

I nod my head. "I'm a good girl," I say because I think that's what he wants to hear. "Was Charlotte a good girl?"

I think he pauses but he doesn't let me go.

"She was weak. Listening to her friends."

Friends. I'm so hoping mine will hurry up and get here. And with that thought comes a sound. It's not loud, like a swishing in the air, and I go still.

"Ricky threatened to tell, didn't he? He was going to tell what you were doing. Report you to the principal and to the police."

"Shut up!" he yells in my ear and the next thing I know I'm airborne, slamming to the floor with a thud. "You don't know anything! That wannabe gang boy thought he could mess with my money. Told Trina to walk away from me. He was the fool, signed his own death warrant the moment he told her to leave me. Killing him wasn't just a necessity. It was actually fun."

My face lies against the cool tile as I let his words register in my mind. He killed Ricky. I try to get up and then I see the tips of Timberland boots in my peripheral and feel relieved.

"You would have lost everything. Your teaching job, your little job on the yearbook, everything. You'd lose everything if the truth came out, wouldn't you, Mr. Lyle?"

Pushing myself up off the floor, I look right into his beady dark eyes. I always thought they were creepy-looking; tonight they're beyond that.

I mean, really, they are. His eyes are completely black now, no whites surrounding the irises, nothing but black. I swallow hard.

He laughs.

"You have no idea, little girl. No idea at all."

Then Mr. Lyle is the one flying across the room, his big body slamming hard against the racks with all the balls. He hits the floor with a thud and everything else falls on top of him.

Run, Krystal. Ricky says from the corner where I saw him.

But I can't move.

I look from Ricky to Mr. Lyle, who's rising from the floor straight upward like a corpse. I open my mouth to scream when I see the desk flying through the air, coming straight at me.

Then there's Jake, his eyes focused on the desk, shifting its trajectory so that it crashes through the window instead. Ricky moves and stands in front of me as another desk floats through the air. Jake can't get this one because Mr. Lyle has turned his attention to him. Now the both of them, with strength unlike anything I've ever seen, are fighting.

The desk is going to hit me, I just know it is. I can see right through Ricky. I know he's not completely crossed over, I know there's nothing he can do to help me, but then...he turns to me and covers me with his body like a shield. There's a loud crashing and the desk falls to the floor.

In the next second Sasha's right beside me. "Krystal, oh, God, you're all right."

"I am," I say and look over to Ricky, who now has that glow around him. Was that how he'd protected me from the desk? Some afterlife shielding powers?

That thought is interrupted by a deep moaning that echoes throughout the entire room. Jake's standing over Mr. Lyle, I guess where he pummeled him to the ground. But Mr. Lyle isn't fighting back anymore, he's lying there, his whole body shaking like he's having some kind of fit.

His mouth is wide open, his eyes, those black pits in the center of his face, shining and then the smoke comes. That thick black smoke I've been seeing for days comes pouring out his eyes, his ears, his nose and his mouth. In long steady streams, it floats upward to the ceiling where it meets and in a dark path goes right out through the broken window.

Me, Sasha and Jake just watch in silence. In fear of what we know is still out there.

thirty

The windows in my room have been rattling since I got out of the tub and sat on the bed, putting lotion on my legs. I try to ignore it.

Turning off the light and slipping under the covers, I take a deep breath and attempt to clear my mind. Tonight has been more than eventful. Jake battered Mr. Lyle badly enough and then that new girl, the one Jake had been trying to get away from at the dance, just appeared. I don't know how long she'd been standing in the doorway; hopefully not long enough to have seen the spirit that left Mr. Lyle's body. But anyway, she used her cell phone to dial 911. Then we all kind of stood in the hallway waiting for the cops to arrive. I don't know how word made it to the dance. I'm thinking the sound of windows breaking and desks slamming against the floor alerted someone. Then a few school staffers had come to see what was going on. At first it looked like they weren't going to believe us. Like for an instant they were going to haul all of us down to the office for beating up a teacher. But then Camy stepped up, crying and ranting about how Mr. Lyle said he was going to make her a big star. That sort of validated our explanation that he was taking pornographic pictures of girls and posting them online. The rest was for the cops to work through.

Then all our parents were called and we had to sit in the teacher's lounge while the police talked to each one of us. My mother and Gerald showed up, both of them flanking me like guardian angels. Although I didn't say it, I was grateful they were there. Both of them.

"How did you know about Mr. Lyle?" the cops asked me.

"He called my cell phone and told me to meet him here. He's been sending me texts and instant messages for a few weeks now."

"And you went, just like that?" Gerald asked, the sound of exasperation in his voice. "Don't you know how dangerous that is? That bastard could've killed you."

"Let her talk, Gerald."

"Mr. Lyle was my teacher. But I didn't know that he was the one calling me. The instant messages were innocent enough. But then the texts came and the pictures. If I would have known all along it was him I would have said something sooner."

After another grueling hour of questioning and explaining, I still wasn't sure the adults believed me. I felt good knowing that Ricky's murderer was being arrested and hopefully given a long jail sentence. Twan and his crew were no longer suspects in his murder. And now Ricky is free to cross over to where he truly belongs.

That brings me to the here and now and these freakin' dead people who insist on coming into my room at night for private conversations. This is going to make keeping the Mystyx secret much harder.

The clacking sound against the window that I'd dismissed as the wind isn't the wind. It's the spirits, knocking, so to speak. I knew this because the room has suddenly grown very chilly. I flip around like a seal until I am lying flat on my back with my hands on my stomach. I probably look like I am playing dead myself when I'm actually trying to concentrate.

I'd read online that one who had the ability to communicate with the dead could also control those communications. So I'm lying here with my eyes closed trying my hardest to communicate.

How do you say *get the hell out* to dead people?

You hear me, I know you do. That's the first time he spoke. I don't know who he is, sounds old. I won't even open up my eyes to look at him because I'm not tryin' to do his bidding right now. If I'm going to do this medium thing then they are going to have to work on my time. I mean, I do have a life—at least now I do.

Over and over I repeat that mantra in my mind—convincing myself that this is how it will be. My breathing is slowing to a steady even rhythm, my mind melding with my body.

It sounds like something's shuffling across the floor, then my bed shakes. He's trying to get my attention.

Drumming my fingers once, I just keep focusing—breathing in deeply, breathing out slowly—in deep, out slow.

Get up, you lazy twit!

In deep, out slow.

I need you to tell Gladys something. That witch is spending my money like it's water. You've got to stop her!

In deep, out slow. In deep, out slow.

Fine! he finally yells. *I'll wait until you call but you'd better not take too long.*

The bed shakes again, so hard my cheeks jiggle. And then there's nothing. The room is quiet and the frigid air seems to have been sucked right out. Cautiously I open one eye, peeking into the darkness to make sure nobody's there.

I don't feel him so it's no big deal that I can't really see anything anyway. Then I smile, right there in my bed, in my dark room all by myself, I smile. I did it!

The spirit is gone, resigned to come back when I call him, when I'm ready to deal with him. I controlled him. He didn't scare me and he didn't tell me what to do. I was the boss.

Flipping back onto my stomach I'm still smiling as I burrow deeper into my pillow and search for sleep.

First, let me just say it's not the infamous walk into the light that everybody likes to describe it as. The actual crossing over from here to eternity involves a lot less fanfare and a lot more emotion than I ever expected.

We're at the cemetery again.

I sure hope I'm not going to spend too much of my time here, but I had to see Ricky off. I'd never feel completely satisfied if I didn't. He has the aura of a spirit now, but he said he still hadn't taken a walk down that path. He hadn't taken that turn in the road like Trina had explained to me.

Ricky said he wanted to do that with me.

His hands are in his pockets and his legs are spread apart—his favorite stance. I smile because I know I'm going to miss seeing that, seeing him, talking to him. I'm going to miss Ricky, period.

I remember the day I met him, the way he looked so confident and arrogant asking for my help. And after all these weeks, when I thought all I wanted to do was ignore these spirits harassing me, I'm wondering if there's any way we can keep in touch. It's weird, I know, but he's become so much more than just a spirit, more than just someone I need to help. I know there's a name for what he is to me, I just can't pinpoint it right now.

"So this is it, huh?" I say, hoping I sound real casual-like. My hands are shaking. I keep trying to make them be still but it's not working.

Yeah, it is.

"Are you scared?"

He shrugs. *Nah. Can't be any worse than living in a world where teachers prey on young girls, mess with them, take pictures of them and then kill them.*

"Well, when you put it like that, I'd have to agree with you."

You're a real cool girl, Krystal.

"Thanks."

I meant what I said about some dude being happy to get you. I've seen you hanging with that weather boy and even though he's not your type, I guess it's okay if you kick it with him for a while.

"Oh, you guess it's okay. Like I need your permission."

Our conversation is light, like we're just standing at the bus stop or something. Nobody would ever guess I'm alive and he's dead and that in a few minutes I'd be heading home to have dinner with my mother and stepfather and he'd be on his way to eternity.

He's laughing and that makes me feel better about letting him go.

I'ma still keep an eye you.

"Please don't." I'm touched that Ricky would even consider watching over me. Thinking back, I shouldn't have gotten attached to a spirit. But emotions are deeper and more persuasive than reason. I liked having Ricky around and I'm trying real hard not to cry because I'll never see him again.

Um, Trina says she's sorry.

That seems out of the blue, but then again it doesn't. It figures that guilt was driving Trina's involvement in what I was doing for Ricky. Actually, I wouldn't have been able to figure that out except for my visits with Dr. Whack Quack. He actually did make some good points sometimes.

"Why didn't she just tell you about Mr. Lyle?"

I guess she was afraid or something. She said she felt like dirt after he posted those pictures. So this is it, he says and kind of looks over his shoulder.

I look, too, because I want to see where he's going. But all I see is the rest of the cemetery. The weather seems to be cooperating today, no heavy winds, no rain, no anything else. The sky is clear, the sun shining. A good day to go home, I guess.

Thanks, Krystal. I really appreciate all you did. Nobody's ever helped me before so I'm not used to this. But I'm glad it was you.

I'm feeling real proud of myself as I clench my hands together in front of me. "I'm glad it was me, too."

And I'll tell the others to cut you some slack, you're new to this ghost whisperer thing and you need time to get adjusted.

"Thanks. I appreciate that."

And then he turns, I see him take a couple steps and then I don't see him anymore. The sensation I've come to relate to Ricky's presence has left me. Ricky has left me.

Alone.

In the cemetery looking like a goofball.

I smile, then I chuckle, then I laugh so hard I have to sit down. My back is against his stone once again and I let my head loll back. I'm in the cemetery and I'm not afraid of ghosts. Instead I'm almost anticipating my next spiritual assignment.

Yeah, and I'll be keeping that little tidbit to myself. Don't want to see Dr. Whack Quack any more than I have to.

thirty-one

It is finally here. The wind howls like a chorus of banshees outside the windows. The temperature has dropped from a seasonable sixty degrees to a bone-chilling thirty-four. And it is snowing.

Yep, it's May 1 and snow is falling from the sky like it was December 1. So far, six inches have already fallen.

I am absolutely amazed. The natives aren't.

Weather anomalies, Franklin has explained. As we, the Mystyx, sit at our lunch table waiting for the school principal to make the decision to close schools early, we wonder what will happen next.

"It's gotta be a sign," Sasha says, taking a bite of her apple. "Pops said every time there's an unexplained weather event in Lincoln, there's a surge in the supernatural power source, a surge in our Power." Sasha has taken to calling Jake's grandfather "Pops," probably because nobody else calls him that. Still I think it is a little presumptuous of her to be that familiar with a member of someone else's family.

I consider what she's just said. The last thing I need is another power surge. I've already accepted my powers as a medium and have even developed some control over my afterlife acquaintances. Then there are the visions. I think

I've had them all along but just dismissed them as elaborate dreams. Now, I can recognize the cold chill and slightly nauseous feeling when I'm about to have one. All of this I've accepted as part of my nature. I'm not all that sure I'm ready for any more just yet.

"Franklin's dad said it seems like a Nor'easter coming down from Canada, except that it normally happens in February, not May. All I know is, I don't want any more power," I say adamantly.

Jake is already shaking his head. He'd gotten a haircut but I don't think he likes it. He keeps rubbing his hand over his forehead like he's missing something there. Using our power on Mr. Lyle sort of brought about a change in all of us.

Sasha seems happier and her mood swings are a little less volatile. She enjoys her new powers, says they make her feel strong and beautiful. I just go along with her because mine don't really make me feel that way.

Jake is still quiet and still looks down at the floor or the table a lot. He's still a Tracker and he's still struggling academically, but when he smiles he looks genuinely happy. When he talks to us he says things about his future that show optimism. He has plans, wants to become a veterinarian.

As for me, well, I'm still me. Only now, instead of wondering how it'll feel to be kissed by a ghost, I like how it feels to be kissed by Franklin.

"Hey, did ya hear they're closing school early?"

She seems to suddenly appear at the table quietly, but her presence always seems to bring something else. Jake looks up at the sound of her voice. Sasha continues to eat but stares at her. I stuff my trash into my lunch bag and wait because we all know she has more to say. She is like that, talkative, all the time.

"So, I was thinking that if you guys aren't doing anything

we could go hang out at my place. Maybe have a snowball fight or something. I've got a killer arm that I can't wait to try out. Plus, it doesn't look like it's going to stop snowing anytime soon so we'll probably be off school tomorrow, too. Why not get a head start on the weekend?"

Her name is Lindsey Yi; she just transferred to Settlemans from out of state. She's the girl from the dance, the one that just about pulled Jake onto the dance floor and the one who appeared after the incident with Mr. Lyle. She hasn't said a word about what happened that night, so I am taking that as a sign that she didn't see anything unusual. I'm sure not going to ask her if she did. Anyway, it is obvious that Jake doesn't like her.

He groans at the sight of her or the rapid-fire words that seem to practically pour from her mouth at any given moment. I don't know which, but it makes me laugh. Then the cafeteria goes into a state of pandemonium. Lindsey has brought us some news and it looks like the rest of the students have just gotten the same announcement.

Before anybody can say another word, we are up and out of the cafeteria, heading straight to our lockers. I've just stepped out of the double doors when Sasha grabs my arm.

"Come on, you're riding with us."

I know enough now not to even argue with her. The bus lets me off at the corner where my house is, Sasha lived in the opposite direction, as does Jake. But I guess since we are now connected by the Power, it makes sense that we stick together all the time.

It's absolutely bone-chilling out here, the wind's blowing snowflakes all over the place. I remember when I was younger I used to like watching the snow fall from the window in our apartment. But that was always so pretty and orderly. This, what is going on right now in Lincoln, is not a neat, pretty snowfall. It seems more like an angry, defiant blizzard.

I can barely see Sasha in front of me and even stumble a few times as the snow is getting deeper. Beside me, Jake takes my elbow, helping to keep me steady. That is something else I am getting used to, Jake always being there to help me out.

I turn to smile at him but can barely see anything besides his tall physique covered in coat, hat, gloves and scarf. We keep walking but I am starting to wonder if we'd passed the car. The parking lot never seemed this far away before. Sasha must have been thinking the same thing because she gasps as I bump into her.

"Sorry," I grumble and think she probably should have said something before simply stopping like that.

"I thought the car was right over here," she says, her voice muffled by the thick purple scarf she wears over her lavender wool coat.

My coat is nice, not quite as nice as Sasha's. It's from Lands' End, and it's wool, too, just not in that cute, form-fitting style. Actually Gerald bought the coat for me and it is a nice charcoal-gray color, very warm inside and very practical. The boxy shape doesn't really matter much as I wasn't going for the fashionista look this morning when I left the house, but the keep-my-body-as-warm-as-possible look instead.

Anyway, the three of us just kind of stand there looking around. I doubt they can see anything other than snow and blinding white, just like me.

"Where's Mouse?" I ask. "Can't you call him on your cell phone?"

"There's no signal," Jake offers. "I tried to call Pop Pop to let him know I was on my way before we left the building. A couple other students said they didn't have any signal either."

"That's great," I huff.

"I think it's that way," Sasha says and we try to stay huddled as close together as possible while following her.

My knees start to hurt and lifting each boot-shod foot to take a step is becoming a chore. The snow is almost up to my knees and it looks like it is actually coming down faster. Jake is close behind me. I can hear his heavy breathing over the whistle of the wind. Sasha is right in front of me, wobbling with each step she takes. She's shorter than me so I figure the snow has to be past her knees, making walking almost impossible.

Squinting, I look up ahead and feel a little jolt in my chest because there's nothing in front of us. Turning my head to look over my shoulder, I notice there's nothing behind us. My heart beats a little faster as I take another step. I can't catch my breath. I try to inhale deeply and a gust of wind comes along and snatches it away. My free hand flies to my chest and my feet stay rooted to the spot. Jake's hand tightens on my arm and I can hear him calling my name, but it's too late.

I might have thought I was just cold, sans the howling wind and whipping snowflakes. But I know better. Like tiny little feet marching up my spine, the chill climbs and climbs before settling at the base of my neck, right over my *M*. My stomach twists and I pitch forward, leaning over just in case the nausea turns into a full-fledged heaving.

My temples ache for like a split second and then I see it.

The sky is pitch-dark. No stars, no nothing. The air is chilly and it's quiet, eerily so. No car sounds, no animal sounds, just nothing. I look in front of me, spin around and look behind me. Nothing. There's no one outside but I think I'm standing in the middle of a street. Not the street I live on and not any one that I've ever seen before. Still it feels familiar. I look up at the houses on the street, not mine exactly but again, familiar. I get the feeling the scene represents anywhere, any town, anyplace.

Fear centers in my belly, bubbling like boiling stew.

The ground sort of shakes and I immediately look down. At first there's nothing there. Just my feet and the asphalt. Then the waves begin, swirling and curling around my boots, up to my ankles. It's back again, that black fog that tried to choke me. Now it's reaching up at me, like fingers clawing their way up my body. I try to move but it's useless. Suddenly the black fog is everywhere, tangling around me, floating over the street, drifting up to the doors of the houses. Overhead I hear the birds. I don't see them but then I don't have to. I know them and I know what they're going to do. I still can't run so I open my mouth to scream but the dark fog jumps down my throat, stealing my voice and entering my body.

I'm shaking like I'm having a seizure, all the while the black fog covers everything. Everywhere.

Another gust of wind hits me and I fall straight back, landing in the snow like I'd intended to make a snow angel. Jake is immediately beside me, Sasha falling to her knees, like, an instant later. Both of them have one of my hands and are looking down at me like I died and came back to life.

I blink once. Twice. Then swallow hard.

"It's coming for us," I finally manage to croak.

Sasha is first to reply. "What? What's coming? Did you have a vision?"

Jake sucks his teeth. "Of course she did. Don't ask stupid questions. What was it, Krys? What did you see?"

I close my eyes even though I much prefer the bright snowfall to what I'd seen the last time I closed them. "It's dark and it's coming. It will kill us all."

"Kill the Mystyx?" Sasha says.

I shake my head, choking back a sob—I so don't want to cry in front of them. But it scared me, the finality of it, the cold, creepy, calculation of its plan. It did more than scare me, it terrified me, and I don't quite know how to convey that to them without completely breaking down.

Jake takes off one of his gloves and rubs his bare hand over my cheek. The skin-to-skin contact feels good, reminds me I'm alive. I find a little courage to say, "Not just the Mystyx. Everybody. Everywhere. It's coming for us all."

* * * * *

QUESTIONS FOR DISCUSSION

1. Do you think that supernatural or paranormal powers exist? Why or why not? And have you experienced some phenomenon that you couldn't explain?

2. In Greek mythology the River Styx formed the boundary between Earth and the Underworld, sometimes called Hades. It has been used as a religious allegory in other literary works, including *The Divine Comedy*. How did you interpret the meaning as it relates to the Mystyx?

3. If you could have a supernatural power, what would it be, and why?

4. If Krystal, Jake and Sasha weren't connected by their power, do you think they would be friends? Why or why not?

5. How would you react to Ricky's request to Krystal to help him find his killer? Do you think she did the right thing by helping him? Could she have done more?

6. Has someone you've known or who was close to you in age died? And if so, how did it affect you?

7. Is Krystal's experience being the new person in high school familiar? Do students in your school form cliques and segregate themselves? How do you handle it?

8. How do you feel Calvin, Krystal's father, handled the way he told his daughter about his new life? Do you

think Krystal was right to be angry with her mother for leaving her father?

9. Do you think Krystal will ever accept Gerald as her mother's husband and her stepfather? Why or why not?

10. What character do you think you identify with most?

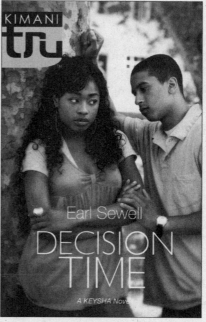